A BRIBE TURNS LETHAL

A
BRIBE
TURNS
LETHAL

A.S. MOST

Visit our website at
www.StillwaterPress.com
for more information.

First Stillwater River Publications Edition.

ISBN: 978-1-965733-38-7

Library of Congress Control Number: 2025900936

1 2 3 4 5 6 7 8 9 10
Written by A.S. Most.
Cover & interior book design by Matthew St. Jean.
Cover assets by thailoei92 and Vector Archive / Adobe Stock.
Published by Stillwater River Publications,
West Warwick, RI, USA.

Publisher's Cataloging-in-Publication
(Provided by Cassidy Cataloguing Services, Inc.)

Names: Most, A. S., author.
Title: A bribe turns lethal / A.S. Most.

Description: First Stillwater River Publications edition. |
West Warwick, RI, USA : Stillwater River Publications, [2025]
Identifiers: LCCN: 2025900936 | ISBN: 9781965733387
Subjects: LCSH: Reporters and reporting—Fiction. |
Investigative reporting—Fiction. | Implants, Artificial—
Complications—Fiction. | Medical supplies industry—
Corrupt practices—Fiction. | Bribery—Fiction. |
Woman-woman relationships—Fiction. | LCGFT:
Detective and mystery fiction. | Thrillers (Fiction) | BISAC:
FICTION / Medical. | FICTION / Thrillers / Medical.
Classification: LCC: PS3613.O7885 B75 2025 |
DDC: 813/.6—dc23

A BRIBE TURNS LETHAL

CHAPTER 1

Harriet Nugent had no difficulty wriggling out of the Uber, but standing erect was a different story. Her daughter, waiting in front of the restaurant they'd chosen for lunch, watched her mother hobble the short distance in obvious discomfort. It pained her to see this vigorous woman she loved move uncharacteristically slowly toward her.

Face-to-face with her daughter, Harriet flashed a warm smile and the two embraced. With the exception of her limiting gait, Harriet was a healthy appearing, well-proportioned woman in her sixties with straight, shoulder-length grey hair. Her daughter, two inches taller at five feet seven, shared her bright-eyed smile, sparkling blue eyes, and slender build. They were an attractive mother-daughter couple.

"Been over a month since I've seen you, Mom. You seem more distressed than you did on our trip to the Met that day."

"Guess so, Leslie. I'm back to where I was four years ago when I went in for hip surgery. Maybe even a little worse in terms of pain when I put any weight on my hip."

"Well, let's find our table in the restaurant, Mom, and take some pressure off that hip."

The meal was excellent; shrimp scampi for Harriet and broiled scallops for Leslie. They caught up on family matters and had just enough time to cab over to Dr. Lindell's office at Metro Hospital for Harriet's two thirty appointment. Leslie was surprised her mother didn't probe her thirty-six-year-old, unmarried daughter's social situation, but attributed that to the distraction of hip discomfort and her apprehension about the gloomy news Lindell was likely to deliver in his office.

Dr. Gene Lindell kept tightly to his schedule. By three thirty, Harriet and Leslie were sitting opposite the handsome physician still wearing a green scrub cap over his black hair with slight traces of gray showing at the temples. The office was standard hospital issue, painted light blue with two Winslow Homer seascape prints on the limited wall space. The only furniture was a small desk and chair for the doctor and two chairs opposite for a patient and someone along for the patient's comfort.

"I'm guessing you have it figured, Harriet. It's the hip. Same one we replaced four years ago. I said it would last ten years at a minimum and probably more like twenty. That's been my experience. You're my first and hopefully only premature failure in twelve years of practice. I can only apologize for your unique status. I think you need another operation."

Harriet's expression didn't convey a sense of disappointment.

"I knew that was coming, Dr. Lindell. I hope a second trip to the OR will have a better outcome."

The surgeon's faint smile offered some sympathy. "I'd count on it, Harriet. Any questions?" He turned slightly to face the daughter. "Ms. Nugent?"

"Like my mom, it's no surprise, but why so early is my only question. Does she have the same hip prosthesis as all your other patients? Will you be inserting the same type as the one that failed? Those are my questions, Doctor."

"My daughter's a newspaper reporter, Dr. Lindell, so she has a reporter's curiosity."

"I welcome her questions. We'll know more if I do the surgery and have the prosthesis in my hand to examine. That'll tell me a lot. Today the original prosthesis is still the hip joint of choice."

Lindell got up, indicating the session was over.

"Harriet, my nurse will help you with any questions you may have about the next steps." He then turned his attention to Leslie. "While your mother is filling out some papers, Ms. Nugent, I wonder if you would just stay back here for a moment?"

Leslie registered mild surprise but stayed in the office as her mother exited with the nurse, who appeared as if on cue.

Lindell put on his most relaxed smile.

"Could I call you for dinner some evening, Ms. Nugent?"

Not surprised by his forward approach, Leslie had sized him up as a straight shooter and a nice-looking guy. She knew guys found her attractive. Briefly considering his request, she thought they might enjoy an evening together. Digging in her purse, Leslie found her card holder and handed a card to him.

"My cell is the only phone on the card. Give me a call."

CHAPTER 2

Looking out the window of his third-floor office, Lester Brandt saw heavy traffic on the West Side Highway. It was slow going in both directions at this late hour of the afternoon. A bit further west, beyond the highway, he could see the boat basin on the Hudson River and a flotilla of twelve small sailboats about to engage in the usual Wednesday five o'clock. race.

He was envious, wishing he was out there competing. Instead, he was cooped up in an office, twirling a pencil, awaiting his fifth meeting of the day. At forty-five, he was vice president for purchasing at a large hospital system, third largest in the States. Metro Hospitals extended beyond New York City into Westchester County, Rockland County, Long Island, and New Jersey.

Still, he wished he could unhook his leash and be free, if only for a few hours, to enjoy the spray in his face as he sailed down the racecourse.

"Mr. Dillon is here for your five o'clock Mr. Brandt." His speakerphone brought him back to earth.

AllCare serviced several large hospital systems. Metro Hospitals was its number one customer and Lester Brandt was the key decisionmaker AllCare's president had to keep happy.

"Send him in, Lorraine, and please bring us a fresh pot of coffee."

Eric Dillon came in with a big smile. Lester rose to greet

him. The two men were similar in age and height. Dillon's build reflected his many hours in a gym. Lester's hair was more gray than blond; Dillon's the reverse but thinning out.

Lester's suit jacket hung on a hook behind the entry door. Dillon took his off and hung it on the same hook. He was quite at home in this office.

"Good to see you, Les. You're looking fit. I can still see the remnant of a tan. Must be left over from that week-long conference in the Caymans."

"Yeah, the weather was perfect, Eric. I even got in two rounds of golf."

"This won't be a very long meeting, Les. I just want to tell you about our last quarter financials. I'm sure you'll be pleased."

"I'm all ears, Eric, so give me the good news."

"Here's the data in a nutshell. Earnings for AllCare were up twelve percent and profit was up seven percent. We had our best quarter ever. In actual numbers that brings our annual sales to six point seven billion with zero point six billion in profit, and half of that profit is due to Metro's business."

Lester gave an appreciative nod and slight smile. For a moment he turned and looked out his window at the sailboat race in the river. He turned back to Eric

"Ever do any sailing, Eric?"

"Can't say that I have. Never cared for the water. I grew up in Wyoming where guns and hunting were the passion, not boats. But you changed the subject, Les. Something on your mind?"

"Just thinking, Eric. I know the news is good. My share of the profit will swell my Cayman account to some obscene number. I'm not unappreciative, Eric, but sometimes I ask myself if that's really what I'm after. I also avoided asking how you increase the profit margin in such a competitive market-place. Maybe I don't want to know the details."

"Don't go soft on me, Les. Our partnership has benefitted each of us beyond our expectations. Enjoy it. Spend some of it on you and your wife. I mean it. And the answer to your question about how we increase our profit margin is simple: we lower our costs."

"I'm sorry for putting a damper on your glad tidings, Eric. See those racing boats out there? I get moody when I see them and wonder why I'm not out there with them doing something I love."

"Damn it, Les. You have a beautiful twenty-eight-foot sailboat. I've been on it. It's magnificent. Stop envying those sailors down there in their little toy boats."

Dillon rose and went for his jacket. Lester followed him to the door.

"Eric, thanks for the kick in the pants. You shook my gloom. I appreciate the way you run the business. This silent partner owes you a lot. Thanks, fella."

CHAPTER 3

The couple stood in a darkened doorway, locked in an embrace, catching their breath after a long passionate kiss.

"I wondered when we'd get around to this," she whispered.

"You knew I was going to kiss you the first chance we got," he answered in a husky voice.

She leaned into him and let her left leg move ever so slightly in between his legs. She felt his growing hardness and it gave her a warm feeling.

"Let's try that kiss again, Jake. We were just getting the hang of it."

They kissed again, this time even longer, and then drew apart breathing heavily.

"We've started down a bumpy road, Angela, but it's a ride I wouldn't wanna miss."

They turned together, arms around each other, and disappeared into the darkness beyond the doorway.

The silence was total, until the audience erupted in applause. The house lights came on; the cast came out for their bows and to enjoy the applause. Ivy Brandt and Ted Swan, the stars who ended the play in the doorway, held hands as they took their curtain calls together.

Backstage the cast was excited by the way the audience had received their opening night offering. Laughter and smiles were abundant. The director and author, Mark Lewis, congratulated each actor individually.

"Ivy, you were terrific. I especially loved that final scene.

You and Ted really nailed it. I think the audience could feel the heat you two generated together."

"Thanks, Mark. That means a lot to me." To herself, she thought about the tingling generated by rubbing against Ted. That was not in the script. Now she wondered if Ted was going to build on the moment. She wanted to find out if he was as hungry as she was for some private time.

Ivy turned to her leading man, still holding his hand. "I'm too excited to head home, Ted. Why don't we break away from the crowd and find a quiet place to reflect on the evening?" Reflection was not what she had in mind.

Ted had to stop and think for a moment. Ivy's invitation had taken him by surprise. After blanking a few seconds, he recovered his composure and responded.

"You know that small hotel down the block, Ivy, the Branville? It looks like just the right place. Why don't we walk on down there and see what we can do about finding that quiet place you were looking for?"

The handsome forty-two-year-old, broad-shouldered leading man was robust. At six feet two he towered over Ivy's five feet five. His sandy colored hair and perfect white teeth gave him the look of a Malibu lifeguard, albeit a few years past prime. Not surprising, since that was where he'd been discovered and hired to play in a daytime TV soap opera. When that gig ended it left him jobless in New York until he was cast in the current play, *Climbing for Love*. Women enjoyed their time with him even though it was usually just a meaningless romp.

The Branville was used to having short-stay guests without luggage. The couple checked in and were out in little over an hour. The sex was rushed but each was excited by the novelty of starting an affair with their attractive costar.

Out on the street, about to hail a cab, they were reflective.

"That was a bit hurried, Ted, but still a hell of a workout. Next time we'll know each other better."

"Ivy, you were terrific. I think we have real chemistry together."

Ivy was married and Ted understood her need for complete secrecy. They looked forward to using the Branville frequently during their engagement up the street.

CHAPTER 4

The reviews she'd read of *Climbing for Love* were enthusiastic, so Leslie considered herself lucky to have gotten two tickets while the play was in its second week. Tonight, she and her friend Diana were applauding madly as the stars took their curtain calls. Diana Gold was good company on a theater night; she stayed awake and actually gave the play serious thought.

"Wow, Leslie. What a performance and what a play! I'm so glad you read the reviews and jumped at the chance to get these tickets."

The small theater was slowly emptying. The two women were patiently waiting their turn to get in the aisle and join the line heading for the exit.

"You know, Leslie, we haven't seen a good drama in quite some time. This one really got to me. The lead couple had great chemistry and made the tragic events seem very real."

"You're a softy, Diana, but I know what you mean. I was near tears when the woman's child died. Sad is hardly the word to describe his death."

Diana stopped Leslie from joining the audience escaping in the crowded aisle.

"I didn't tell you, Leslie, but I know Ivy Brandt. We were in the same sorority at Michigan, over ten years ago. We haven't spoken to each other since that long-ago time of life, but I bet she'll remember me. I'm gonna try to see if she'll speak with us backstage. Maybe even go for a drink."

"Worth a try, Di. I'd love to meet her, especially after seeing her in a lead role."

They eventually maneuvered through the crowd and ended up in front of the stage. Ivy Brandt was animated as she spoke to a small group of fans. Over the heads of her admirers, she saw Diana and flashed a quick smile.

"We're in luck. She recognized me. Let's give her a minute to break away. You're not in a rush, are you Leslie?"

"Not at all. I'd enjoy meeting her."

Ivy finally escaped and came over to greet Diana.

The blue-eyed blond with a short pageboy haircut moved gracefully; her slim figure well-maintained by daily workouts. She was quick to smile and flash her perfect teeth.

"Hard to believe I'm seeing you, Di. It's been a lifetime. I knew you in an instant. How the hell are you? And who is your friend?"

"Ivy, this is Leslie Nugent, a very good friend. She's a reporter with *the Times*."

Leslie gave Ivy a broad smile and extended her arms as an expression of awe. She offered effusive praise. "You'd have earned a rave review if I was a critic, Ivy. You were great."

"Why thank you, Leslie. That's awfully kind."

Diana stepped in and took charge. "Can Leslie and I take you out for a drink?"

Ivy liked the suggestion. "Great idea, Diana. Leon's Bar and Grill just down the block is a perfect place. Take a left out the door. I'll meet you there in twenty minutes. That'll give me time to change clothes and decompress. Okay?"

Diane and Leslie nodded in agreement and headed off to Leon's.

The tavern was like dozens in the village; dimly lit with a long mahogany bar at the back of a large room. A huge mirror, missing a lot of silver backing, ran along the wall behind the bar. The customary array of liquor bottles and glassware fronted the mirror. Backless barstools with worn brown leather seats completed the scene. Tables with simple wooden chairs lined the two side walls. A few tables with chairs occupied the center of the room.

Diana picked out a table along a wall and they settled in. The mild autumn night had spared them the need for coats; light coverings sufficed and didn't have to be hung up. The bartender took note of them as did the three or four male patrons seated at the bar. Leslie told the bartender a third person would be joining them, and they would order drinks when she got here.

Diana could hardly wait to sit down before she began talking. "I don't know how long Ivy's twenty minutes will last so let me fill you in quickly on our drinking buddy. Ivy Bayliss grew up in rural Michigan. She was an all-state soccer star in high school and came to Michigan on a soccer scholarship. Her family had three kids and could barely make ends meet working a small farm. The scholarship was crucial. As a soccer star she played rough but could take it as well as she dished it out; maybe soccer was the release that let her be amiable off the field.

"Not surprisingly, the beautiful blond athlete was heavily rushed by several sororities. When she chose us, we considered it a big deal. Ivy was well-liked and elected house president in our senior year. She didn't have any really close friends. She dated lots of guys, but I don't remember her taking any of them seriously.

"She could be a nasty enemy if you got in her crosshairs. I've got an anecdote to share with you when we have more time.

"In her junior year she was bitten by the theater bug; quit soccer and took up acting in a serious way. She gave up her athletic scholarship and had to make up the money taking jobs on campus and in Ann Arbor. When we graduated, she headed east to pursue an acting career. That's where we lost contact. I see her heading our way, so I'll stop here."

Ivy's entrance into Leon's drew the attention of the scattered males in the tavern. Dressed simply in a skirt and sweater with a short leather jacket, she was a knockout. She spotted her friends and cruised right over, sporting the same big smile she'd beamed in the theater. She grabbed a chair and beckoned the bartender over to their table.

Ivy and Diana didn't take long to start reminiscing about old school days. The drinks were quick to arrive; three margaritas with lots of salt on the rims.

"What are you doing, Di? Last I remember you were considering law school."

"You have a good memory, Ivy. I finished law school at Michigan and joined a small firm of women lawyers here in New York. We specialize in divorce law and have clients of both genders. I enjoy the work and believe me, it's challenging.

"I'm single now. My husband, Will, was killed in Afghanistan while working as a war correspondent for *Time* magazine. We didn't have children. That was five years ago. It took several years before I could put Will's death behind me and resume life as a single woman."

"Oh, Diana. So sorry to hear about Will."

Ivy reached out and placed a hand on Diana's shoulder. Her face expressed genuine sympathy for her old friend.

She next focused on Leslie. "What about you, Leslie?"

"My story is fairly simple, Ivy. I have a dream job. I've been a newspaper reporter ever since I graduated college, first in Washington, D.C. and now at *the Times*. I've had two serious romances with guys rooted in careers too far away to get us over the finish line. I love my work and wonder if that's part of the problem...if there *is* a problem. In any event, I'm very single."

Ivy smiled. "And enjoying it, I suspect. Good job, good looks, and a great city. The trifecta."

"You're last, Ivy," said Diana. "That gold band on your left hand says you've crossed the goal line."

"Not once, but twice, Di. I'm married to a hospital executive. My first marriage was very brief and ended in divorce. Nuff said about *that* misadventure."

Leslie and Diana were interested in hearing about life in the theater and kept the actress answering questions for the next half hour through a second round of drinks. Finally, Ivy had to beg off.

"Girls, you'll have to forgive me. This has been great, but sleep is a high priority during the play's run."

Ivy abruptly got up and slipped on her jacket. "I've got to run but let me have your business cards. You never know when a friendly divorce lawyer will come in handy, Di."

Ivy pocketed the cards, blew Diana a kiss, and gave a friendly wave to Leslie. She was halfway to the door before they could get up to say goodbye.

Leslie's smile was one of curiosity. Her reporter instinct was picking up an undercurrent in Ivy's closing remark. "I got the feeling that her reluctance to reflect, even briefly, on her current marriage may have tied into that final comment on using a friendly divorce lawyer."

"Leslie, I know better than to challenge your ability to sniff out stories when the scent is even too weak for canines to pick up on it."

"Hey, I'm only grasping for a straw. She was very nice and even allowed us to pick up the tab for her drinks. She sounds interesting and could be a character in a book I was writing, if I was writing a book."

"Well, maybe we'll all meet again, and you'll have a chance to find out how close your imagination was to reality. Think about how we might get together and let her dig a bit deeper into *our* less than exciting lives."

CHAPTER 5

Lester Brandt came home to a darkened apartment. He knew Ivy was working tonight so he ate supper alone at a Japanese restaurant near his office on upper Broadway.

He'd put in a long and tiring day. Having this time to himself was a welcome breather. He poured a glass of Black Label over ice and settled into the very comfortable Eames chair in the dimly lit living room. Lester didn't expect Ivy home before eleven, so he had at least two hours to reflect on the day's events.

Lester grew up in Scarsdale, New York, the only son of divorced parents. After college at Williams and business school at Yale, he studied health care administration at Columbia. Upon completing an administrative residency at a small hospital in Connecticut, he joined the Metro Hospital system as assistant to the vice president in charge of purchasing at their flagship hospital in New York City. After four years he replaced his boss when the latter moved to a senior management position in Chicago. Lester's ascent had taken place very quickly due to a combination of serendipity and ability. Now he seemed anchored in his position.

The one negative in his life was the failure of his marriage to Ivy. They met during his administrative residency when she was a struggling actress recently out of acting school. The chemistry was there but that was all. It wasn't enough.

He was solitary and she was very social. His work was fully satisfying and soon began to crowd her out of his life as he experienced professional success. He mused that they had grown apart and were now each privately wondering how to end the marriage amicably. Ivy was undoubtedly looking for affection and Lester wondered if she'd found it with a colleague in her theater crowd. He'd found an outlet for *his* muted passion with one of his assistants, Cheryl Winter.

For Lester, divorce made sense, but making a large payment to get out of the marriage was not something he was willing to concede. He'd been hiding assets in an offshore bank account and had no intention of letting Ivy grab a piece of it. Off-the-books payments from Eric Dillon and AllCare were his cache. No one else knew about his sizable, growing accumulation; most certainly not his wife. He and Ivy lived comfortably on his hospital salary, and he never used his other income to upscale their living style.

He knew Ivy would want a large settlement from the divorce. Her income from acting was quite modest and she'd grown accustomed to a lifestyle in New York that depended on a sizable income stream. A third marriage for her was a possible solution but he suspected she considered that an unattractive option.

CHAPTER 6

Diana's office was quiet at this late hour, closing in on ten o'clock. The six other attorneys in the practice had long ago headed home. No attraction awaited her in her one-bedroom apartment; no husband, no cat or dog. She'd gotten over feeling sorry for herself about Will's death but hadn't been able to get back into the singles dating scene. She was just lonely.

Her phone vibrated and indicated the caller was Ivy Brandt. The caller's identity was a surprise. She had just seen Ivy a few days ago after a hiatus of many years. She didn't expect a follow-up call so soon.

"Hi, Ivy. I really enjoyed meeting you after the play. I'm sorry you had to dash away before we learned more about your life in the theater. What's up?"

"Diana, I feel awkward approaching you, but I feel I can trust you to be as private as I need you to be. It was serendipitous that we reconnected after all these years. I want to hire you to initiate divorce proceedings against my husband, Lester. I think he's having an affair and I want hard evidence of that. I think that may help get me a generous divorce settlement. Can I hire you?"

"Let's slow down a minute, Ivy. I work for a law firm and I'm very busy. I can recommend one of the other six lawyers in the firm. We're all expert on divorce settlements. If any one of us takes on your case, you'll be well-represented."

"I understand, Diana, but I know *you* and want to have

you represent me. I'll be patient. I respect your busy sched-ule. Just say yes and we can go forward on a timetable that works for *you*. My husband is clever, so he won't be easy to trip up."

"Okay, okay, Ivy. For old times' sake, I'll do it. My office will send the necessary papers over to you for your signature. And Ivy, I'm sorry to hear about the marriage coming apart."

"I appreciate your sympathy and your willingness to help, Diana. This has been brewing for several years, and I'm finally ready to face the reality of a loveless arrangement."

"One warning, Ivy, infidelity doesn't carry a lot of weight in divorce court. Not the way it used to. It's too common in failing marriages so judges don't dole out big bucks just because one of the parties has found an outlet for their 'unre-quited passion.'"

"I understand, Diana. I just think that I'd rather go into the divorce negotiation with more than just regret over a loveless marriage. A touch of infidelity can't hurt, can it?"

"Okay, Ivy, I'll put one of our investigators on the prowl and see what he can come up with."

"Thanks a lot, Diana. Having you in my corner is very reassuring."

CHAPTER 7

Alyssa Ross gently tapped her wineglass with a small spoon. The well-dressed crowd quieted and turned toward her.

"I'm so pleased with the turnout this evening. If I may read anything into your response to my invitation it's that you feel as I do, that Dawson Nichols should be our next district attorney for Manhattan. This fundraiser will go a long way to convert that hope into a reality. Dawson's seven years as an assistant DA here in Manhattan have enabled him to establish a remarkable record as a crime-fighter. The handout lists his accomplishments so there's no need for me to detail his tireless activity on our behalf. Dawson is here tonight and would like to meet many of you. A little later he'll say a few words about his agenda when he assumes that most important office. For now, enjoy the food and drink and meet the candidate."

Alyssa picked up her drink and moved into the crowd of her guests. Hosting a fundraiser for a critical officeholder in her tastefully decorated duplex apartment made good business sense. She wanted Dawson Nichols to know who she and her friends were and that their support would be most helpful in his campaign. The invitees were well-heeled, successful business people who could afford to be generous when she made an appeal to support a cause she was backing.

Alyssa was born into wealth in 1967 and, upon her father's death in 2010, succeeded him as president and CEO of Ross-Wagner, one of the largest international shipping companies in the world. Her mother had predeceased her father by twenty years in a private airplane crash in the Caribbean. Alyssa, an only child, was doted on by her father who considered her both his son and daughter. He educated her as a teenager in all aspects of the shipping business in preparation for the day when she would succeed him as head of the company.

A tall woman at five feet seven, Alyssa had an athletic figure. Shoulder-length, straight brown hair framed an attractive face with dark green eyes and few wrinkles. Her mouth upturned slightly at the corners, giving the faint impression of a smile. She looked a good deal younger than her fifty-five years. Nearly thirty of them she'd spent happily married to Victor Taylor, a prominent surgeon; the couple successfully managed two independent careers.

Known to only a very select few, Alyssa also inherited a large illegal drug business in the Metropolitan New York area. Her father had earned his first fortune in drug trafficking. This had allowed him to get into the legitimate shipping business. Alyssa delegated management of the drug activity to trusted lieutenants but kept tight control over the finances. Money laundering was a challenge for anyone dealing with illicit drugs so she had also inherited that headache. These businesses weren't all she'd inherited from her father; she also inherited his capacity to engage in illegal practices without giving a second thought.

Her only child, Letitia, married Eric Dillon in 2015 at the age of twenty-five. She was an accomplished cellist, played in a well-known string quartet and gave private lessons to select students. Alyssa was determined to keep Letitia far removed from the unsavory activities her mother engaged in.

Before Letitia's wedding, a cousin of Alyssa's and senior partner in a large hedge fund suggested she buy a small medical supply company held by his fund. He considered it a "sleeper." He knew Alyssa was looking for a business situation that would allow the young couple to start married life independent of Alyssa's business interests. She discussed this option with Eric and Letitia. They welcomed the opportunity. That was Alyssa's wedding present to the couple. Under Eric's management it had grown into a very large medical supply company called AllCare. Eric's background in the import business played well in the medical supply field.

Alyssa and Eric maintained close contact regarding certain matters involving AllCare's finances. She saw the company as a valuable pathway to launder part of the cash flow generated by her drug enterprise.

CHAPTER 8

Metro Hospital had an annual gala for the surgical staff to attract large donors. Leslie Nugent came as the guest of one of the hospital's anesthesiologists. They were longtime friends from childhood.

Leslie recognized Ivy Brandt and wound her way through the crowd to say hello. She hoped the actress would recognize her after their very brief meeting when she and Diana had met Ivy after the play.

"Ivy, how nice to meet you again." Leslie reintroduced herself, "Leslie Nugent, Diana's friend. We met briefly after your stunning performance several nights ago. I'm here with a friend and staff member who seems to have gotten lost with our drinks."

Ivy took a second to recall the meeting but quickly recovered. "Yes, of course, the reporter. Now it all comes back. I was sorry to leave in such a rush that night."

Leslie steered the conversation into comfortable territory. "Does it look like your show is going to have a long run, Ivy? The reviewers seem to think so."

"We haven't heard anything about that but there hasn't been any talk about shutting down after a short run, either. I guess I'm optimistic."

Lester Brandt suddenly appeared at his wife's side. A tall, handsome, suntanned man with a smile spread broadly across his face. He put his arm around Ivy's waist. She made the introduction and Lester extended his hand to shake Leslie's.

Some light banter followed but Leslie could feel his eyes on her. Her black, sleeveless cocktail dress was quite modest, displaying a minimum of cleavage, yet his eyes hinted at his interest. She added that to her imagined profile of the Brandt marriage.

Leslie was drawn into conversation with Lester about hospital matters. Ivy managed to slip away.

Eric Dillon was a guest of Lester Brandt. Eric's wife didn't enjoy these parties since she didn't know any of the doctors or their spouses. She let Eric out on a long leash while she enjoyed a quiet evening at home watching the TV programs of her choice. He enjoyed his freedom and tried to pick out a wife or date who seemed bored or ignored. He spotted Ivy standing alone and headed over to her. For the moment at least she was by herself and enjoying her drink apart from the crowd.

"Mind if I share some of this solitude?"

Ivy turned to face the man who had approached her from behind. She saw a pleasant looking, middle-aged guy wearing a very well-tailored, double-breasted blue suit. He looked prosperous and didn't look like any doctor she'd ever met at one of these parties. He seemed sober so she saw no harm in being friendly.

"I enjoy a quiet moment alone at these affairs. I charge my battery before wading back into the crowd. I'm Ivy Brandt." She extended her hand and shook his.

"Not related to Lester Brandt, are you?"

"You picked up on that in a hurry. I don't recall seeing you at any of the parties."

"You might have, but I'm not a doctor. I'm Eric Dillon. I sell medical supplies to the hospital. Quite a few I might add."

"So, you're a salesman. A rep. Do I have that right?"

"Close. I own AllCare, the company that supplies Metro

Hospitals with a great many of its medical supplies and devices. I'm sure you'd like me to tell you all about our product lines, but I'm more interested in you and why you sought shelter here away from the madding crowd."

"I guess I'm not the social dynamo some may think I am. A bit of solitude feels good occasionally. And how about you? No shy wallflower. You had no trouble singling me out."

Dillon found Ivy difficult to read. She didn't brush him off but didn't send any positive signals either. He tried a neutral tack, mindful that her husband was a valuable colleague.

"This peaceful isolation may not last very long, Mrs. Brandt, so why don't we have lunch some day this week and find out if we have anything else in common? Lester and I are good friends. I don't think he'll be offended."

"For a 'good friend' Mr. Dillon, you're expecting my husband to look the other way while you cozy up to his wife. Seems a bit brash to me. I'll have to take a pass on your *friendly* invitation. My life is complicated enough right now without adding lunch with an associate of my husband."

Dillon could be reckless, but Ivy was not so inclined. His subtle hit on her came as no surprise. She was aware that men found her attractive and misread her as easy prey.

With that she turned away and dissolved into the crowd. Dillon was left to admire her as she sauntered away without any effort to be especially alluring. She didn't have to try; it just came naturally.

Leslie, feeling a bit like an outsider and seeing her "date" now monopolized in conversation by Lester Brandt, caught a glimpse of Ivy and waded through the crowd to speak to her.

"Ivy, do you have a moment? I enjoyed meeting you the other evening and wondered if you might be interested in spending an afternoon with me just getting to know each other. We could bum around the Village and have lunch."

"A playdate sounds like a great idea, Leslie. I like to get to the theater around five so that would give us plenty of time if we met around noon. How about Thursday? Meet at the Crown Bake Shop in Soho?"

"That works for me, Ivy. I'm looking forward to it."

With that, Ivy flashed a smile, gave an affirmative nod, and headed over to the bar for a refill. Leslie was pleased that her invitation had been so readily accepted. She sensed that Ivy welcomed the opportunity to meet a new friend.

When the evening ended, Leslie reacquired her "date" and they took a cab to her apartment building. They parted with a friendly kiss on the cheek and after he saw her safely into her building the cab continued on to his apartment.

Leslie undressed and got into her pajamas, but before putting out her light, she called Diana. She knew Diana was very likely awake even at twelve thirty in the morning. She rarely turned in before one.

"Hey, Diana. Guess who just met your old friend Ivy at a Metro gala?"

"No surprise, Leslie, given that her husband is a VP at Metro. Did she remember you?"

"Yeah, she recognized me. We spoke briefly but she added to my imagined marriage scenario. Just thought you might want to know." Lastly, she mentioned Lester's appraising eyes.

"I know you like to build a story up from little scraps, Leslie. I can't take issue with anything you've said, trouble is it's not based on anything of substance. You may be proven right someday. Who knows?"

She couldn't tell Leslie about her call from Ivy and that facts were beginning to bear out Leslie's construct about the Brandt marriage.

"One last thing, Diana. I made a date with Ivy to spend an

afternoon together. I didn't include you because I know your days are jammed full of work."

"That's fine, Leslie. You girls go ahead and play together. I'll be busy playing shark for some vengeful wife."

"Just wanted you to know, Di."

"Gotta turn in now, Les. Let me know how it turns out."

Leslie was finding it increasingly difficult to retreat into sleep. People were forever telling her that she had it all, yet she didn't see herself that way. Growing up in middle-class comfort, finding it easy to excel in school, being popular with her peers, and finding romance, albeit short-lived, in a succession of desirable men, she had every reason to feel good about herself.

Good looks, a sense of humor, and a healthy sexual appetite combined with an interesting career made a complete package. Nevertheless, now in her mid-thirties she was increasingly aware of being lonely. All of her enviable attributes didn't make up for the absence of a person in her life in whom she could confide, count on to be there and put her trust in, no matter what the situation confronting her. She also wanted that other person to feel the same way about her. She was prepared to take that pledge; all she needed was for the right person to walk into her life. She and Diana were close but her tragic loss and total immersion in her work were obstacles too difficult for Leslie to surmount.

Dwelling on her situation late at night was hardly productive of change but it was an effective hypnotic. She found the bed lamp switch and was on her way to tomorrow.

CHAPTER 9

Late afternoon: Gene Lindell's office waiting room was packed. After a full morning in the operating room, he considered office hours a relaxing interlude in a busy day of damaged knees and hips.

The patient's digital X-ray was up on a computer screen in the patient's examination room. He had undergone a total hip replacement four years ago and was now experiencing pain in the area of the surgery. Lindell saw worrisome signs on the X-ray consistent with instability of the prosthesis. His examination of the patient told him the same bad news.

Lindell was disturbed to again be seeing failure of the joint so soon after surgery. He told patients the device was good for a minimum of ten years, and, depending on how hard they stressed the joint, more likely to last twenty years or more. Seeing failure again after only four years was disappointing, to say the least.

This would be his second premature joint failure. Harriet Nugent was his first. He explained the problem and told the patient that it looked like the joint would have to be replaced. He commiserated with him, explaining that this was the earliest he had ever had to recommend a "redo" procedure. The patient was seventy-two and thought he might be able to reduce his activities and get along without surgery. Understandably, he was not a satisfied customer when he left.

Gene was troubled by this second early failure; he was

barely able to put it behind him and finish up his office schedule.

One failure he could accept as a fluke, but two could not be ignored. Especially after almost a decade without a failure. Maybe *that* was the fluke?

Gene had many patients with older implants and no failures. They all had received the Arnett hip prosthesis. He'd started practice twelve years ago but these two failures dated back to surgeries only four years ago. Most of his patients had a longer than five-year head start compared with these two and there'd been no failures. It didn't make sense.

CHAPTER 10

During the run of her play, Ivy was out late every night. Lester reflected on that fact and couldn't help but think it was a good setup for her to have an affair. True, their marriage was lacking in intimacy, but that alone wasn't enough to trigger the suspicion in him that Ivy might be playing around during her late evenings. He knew she enjoyed sex and wouldn't have any difficulty finding a willing mate in her pool of aspiring actors. Tonight, he decided to check on her after-theater activity.

The play ran two hours and ended around ten. The theater was a short twenty-minute cab ride from their apartment. Ivy rarely got home much before midnight so there was plenty of time to dally. Tonight, he would observe what she did in the hours before returning home.

Dressed in casual clothes, he positioned himself where he could see the cast emerge from the theater. He was not likely to be seen, much less recognized.

The theater patrons came pouring out at ten after ten, chattering away in a seemingly pleased mood. Ten minutes after that, cast members straggled out the side entrance into an alley leading to the street. Ivy emerged shortly thereafter and quickly attached herself to the arm of one of the male cast members. Lester recognized the actor as Ivy's costar. He'd seen the play on opening night.

People dispersed in all directions. Cabs and Ubers were quickly gobbled up by patrons and cast members. Ivy and her companion headed up the street on foot and abruptly disappeared into the Branville Hotel. Lester quickly followed them and saw the couple, arm-in-arm, enter the elevator. He'd seen enough.

What had been a vague suspicion was now a hardened fact. Ivy was having an affair with a guy who was a fellow cast member. He felt no emotion. That surprised him but on reflection he realized it was consistent with the fact that their marriage had been drained of feeling for each other.

He knew that extramarital activity was almost *de rigueur* in divorce cases so he doubted it would seriously affect a settlement, but it couldn't hurt. He felt somewhat relieved to know that she was coming to the table as a cheating wife, an odd emotion to experience when you caught your wife on her way to bed with another man.

The trip to the theater had been more satisfying than if he'd gone inside to watch the play.

CHAPTER 11

Lester and Cheryl Winter made good use of his many trips away from New York. Jaunts to the Caymans to attend conferences related to hospital products were rather common in the winter. They would book separate flights, and separate rooms (his being free, courtesy of the program sponsor) and avoid any public displays of affection at the resort hotels. As with his apartment in New York, he was scrupulous about avoiding situations that could reveal his affair with Cheryl. When making introductions, Cheryl was a colleague who worked in the same department at Metro Hospital. For the most part this deception was successful.

The investigator Diana assigned to follow Lester was not having any luck snapping pictures of him in a compromising situation. There were moments that raised questions regarding a female companion, but these were few and far between. In New York, Lester would disappear during his lunch break and prove impossible to tail. All in all, there was Ivy's suspicion and nothing to back it up. It was as if Lester knew he was being watched and was too clever to be caught.

All this careful evasion came to naught once Cheryl concluded that there was no future for her in Lester's life. She was a good playmate for him, but staying out of sight and using his careful evasive maneuvers was wearing on her. She also sensed that he was unlikely to make a commitment to her, or any woman, if he felt he could satisfy his needs without out a permanent arrangement.

She suspected Lester was doing banking business on their trips to the Caymans, but he never said a word to her about such activity. On shopping trips into the duty-free town market, his side trips to the same bank were purportedly only to get cash for purchases. Credit cards were welcome everywhere, so she believed he was doing something else. And that activity was important enough to keep scrupulously secret from her. It was the secrecy that convinced her she was onto something big.

Cheryl decided that the best she could do was use the information she'd gathered to facilitate his wife's divorce settlement and then share in that settlement. Her suspicion about the banking activity could be quite valuable to Ivy, although exactly *how* valuable was anyone's guess. Then she'd walk away from Lester and begin a new life. She called Ivy to set up a meeting.

"You don't know me, Mrs. Brandt. My name is Cheryl. I'm a colleague of your husband at Metro. I'm aware that you and Lester are having marital problems and may be considering divorce."

Ivy started to interrupt, but Cheryl cut her off. "Let me finish. I think I can be of considerable help to you in that matter and would like to discuss it with you."

Ivy's curiosity was aroused so she decided to play along.

"Cheryl, I don't know what your angle is here. You may have information that would be helpful to me in the event there was a divorce. I can't imagine what that information might be. Why don't we meet so I can hear what you have in mind? How about lunch at Chez Louis on First Avenue and 22nd Street? Just pick a day when you can get free for an hour."

They settled on a date.

CHAPTER 12

Gene Lindell had been uncomfortable contemplating a date with the daughter of a patient. Friends told him there was no ethical issue as long as he was dating the *daughter* and not the *mother*. He knew that, but hearing it from a friend or two eased his mind.

He was divorced for nearly seven years and had been fixed up frequently in the first few years after the divorce. In recent years fewer and fewer women were sent his way. The many failed hookups had taken their toll. His referring friends and relatives began to see him as either not interested or just unwilling to go the extra distance needed to make a date into something more than a polite meal or theater experience.

Tonight, the date was of his own making. Leslie had accepted his offer over the phone and told him she'd been looking forward to his call. She'd made him feel good and they hadn't even spent any time together.

O'Shea's Pub in Chelsea was a good place to start. It was unpretentious but the food was surprisingly good and the beer selection excellent. She'd indicated that beer was high on her list of friendly evening starters. He liked that.

Gene picked her out easily since she was sitting alone in a booth with a bottle of Blue Moon half emptied into a glass. He slid in opposite her before she could get up to greet him.

"Gene Lindell, Leslie. Glad we could get together." They shook hands across the table.

"And I'm Leslie Nugent, Gene. At least we know we're

meeting the people we meant to see. No IDs needed." They laughed about the formal identification.

"I've never been here before and can see why you picked this place. It's friendly and has a warm feel. I like it already and have only had three beers." She put up her hands in mock surrender. "I'm kidding about the beers. This is my first." She flashed a smile, and he was already glad he'd made the date.

Gene had a youthful look. All in all, he made a good first impression. She knew he was forty-four years old and seven years divorced without children.

He'd been pleased with first impressions before but was often let down in subsequent conversation. In this case, he thought, Leslie would have to descend a long way to let him down. She was good to look at. A slim five feet seven inches, Leslie had a warm smile, full lips, and grey eyes. Her shoulder-length brunette hair was worn straight with bangs.

"Leslie, I'm gonna have a brew and get you a second one if you're ready. Then we can dig into each other's past for some basic bio stuff. I know you're a reporter at *The Times*, recently settled in New York. Never married. I did do an abbreviated search on Leslie Nugent."

The waitress came over, took their drink orders, and left two menus.

"My turn to show how much *I* know, Gene. You're a native of Massachusetts who did his college and med school at Yale. You're an orthopedic surgeon and did your training at Columbia. You've been in practice for about twelve years. That's my entire book on Gene Lindell. Your turn. This is interesting with the two of us spilling the beans about the other."

"Okay, Les. You came here from the D.C. area where you were a news reporter for several years. A big story about the White House got you to *the Times*. You're a Long Island girl even though you've been away from the New York area for much of your adult life. That's not a lot of background, but it'll do for now."

"Gene, I've made many friends in New York, male and female, but I'm not romantically involved now. I love my job. Trying to ferret out good stories is a challenge, but this city is rich in material."

"I don't know if I could be the source of any material, Leslie, but if you see an opening where I can be of any use, give me a chance."

"What I know about doctors and hospitals is limited to what I see on the tube and read in an occasional novel. If you come across any homicidal doctors, zombie doctors, or doctors doing unethical things of consequence, ring me up. I'm a quick study and can build a story out of very little, if given a lead."

"You're on."

The evening was a success on all fronts. The food was good, and they each found the other to be an attentive listener. Gene was easy to talk to and seemed genuinely interested in her private life. He was honest about his failed marriage, sharing the blame with his ex. He admitted it had been a poor match that became more apparent as time passed. Now, he said, he was cautious where romancing women was concerned.

The talk was more intimate than one would expect on a first date, but each had disarmed the other and let a bit of their real selves show. He picked up the tab and they then took a walk through Soho. It was a mild fall evening, just perfect for walking and talking. They held hands as they went, which each took as an indication that they were likely to see each other again. They Ubered to her apartment building where he let her out. They parted thinking "second date." Leslie acknowledged his charm but wasn't sure about their chemistry. *Too soon to tell,* she thought.

CHAPTER 13

The prospect of telling *another* patient that her hip prosthesis had failed prematurely was discomforting. Gene knew it wasn't the fault of the surgeon, unless you considered the choice of prosthesis which *was* the surgeon's responsibility. After years of trouble-free hip replacements, the Arnett hip was now a major problem. He was seeing his third early failure.

The patient's joint replacement had been done a little over four years ago, at the urging of her husband. Now she felt unstable and uncomfortable when walking. The operation had been uneventful. He recalled her case vividly. After two days in the hospital, she went home for rehab. Lindell saw no need for Joan to go to a rehab facility. The physical therapist went to her home and got her started on a program of exercises, supplemented after two weeks by regular visits to a physical therapy facility near her home. Rehab had been a total success. Now, this new pain was limiting her activity.

Gene informed the chief of orthopedics about the recent failures, and they agreed on a moratorium for using the Arnett hip. Purchasing was instructed to stock a new hip prosthesis for surgeons in the department.

CHAPTER 14

The two women sat in a quiet corner of Chez Louis. The popular French restaurant was only sparsely occupied after the midday lunch crowd moved out. It had a cozy feel with dark wooden beams on the ceiling and a dark tile floor. The stucco walls were decorated with watercolors of Parisian scenes. Traditional white tablecloths completed the ambiance. Lunch menus were scanned while each sized up the other. Ivy saw an engaging, somewhat heavily made-up brunette with a good figure. Cheryl saw an attractive blond in a stylish workout suit. They ordered iced teas and salad plates.

"Okay, Cheryl. Let me hear what you have in mind."

"Is it okay if I call you Ivy?"

"Sure. Just get on with the reason for this luncheon."

"Well, this may come as a big surprise, but your husband and I have been seeing each other for several years. I can't say I've enjoyed it, aside from the sex, which has been pretty good. Lester is so intent on keeping our affair secret that he pushes the envelope when it comes to deception and complicated arrangements for our meetings. I've come to the conclusion that even if there is a divorce he won't be making me the next Mrs. Brandt.

"That being the case, I want a generous payout. I figure you may be having trouble getting the goods on his infidelity so I'm looking to give you that evidence in exchange for a piece of your future divorce settlement. That's what this luncheon is all about. I also have information about his financial picture that may be *quite* valuable to you *and me* if we can come to some kind of understanding."

Ivy was seething. She was stunned at how little she knew about her husband's life outside their marriage. But now she was being brought up-to-date by this concubine. The temptation was to reach across the table and throttle the bitch. The only restraint was the offer of insider information that could prove valuable.

She stayed cool and played along. "So, you help me nail him with his infidelity and tell me about some buried treasure. And I pay you back when the check comes. Is that it?"

"In a nutshell, Ivy. I'm not greedy. I'll settle for ten percent. I'm assuming the financial information will be news to you so you should be kindly disposed to the source."

Ivy was quiet while she digested the offer and its proposed cost.

"I assume you have some hard evidence about his infidelity that'll stand up in divorce court."

"I've been planning this for a while so you can be sure the evidence is pretty solid. The financial stuff is less complete, but I think your attorney will make good use of what I have. You also should keep your nose clean so there isn't any offsetting evidence of infidelity coming the other way. That's your call, Ivy."

"It sounds like you have a clue that there is some evidence of infidelity on my part. Has Lester hinted at that?"

"The simple answer is yes. I haven't heard any details, but he seems pretty sure you've been stepping out. Have you, Ivy? If so, have you been as careful as he's been?"

"That's further than I care to go today, Cheryl. Let me think about your proposal. Leave me your phone number. I'll get back to you."

With that, Ivy got up, walked to the cash register, paid

their bill and left. Cheryl sat there wondering if her ship was maybe coming in.

Ivy had no intention of sharing any settlement with Lester's mistress. She'd suspected him of fooling around but it seemed he'd gone further down that road than she'd imagined. The most interesting revelation was the financial information she'd been totally unaware of; a pot of gold to go after. She wondered where that money came from.

She needed to end her trysts with Ted at the Branville. He'd be disappointed. Her tracks had to be as invisible as Lester's. Cheryl's warning had been worth the price of the lunch. For Lester, the cat was out of the bag; the evidence was already out there and in the hands of his vengeful mistress. His buried treasure had captured her attention. Lester screwing this bimbo took a distant second place to his closely guarded cache.

CHAPTER 15

If Gene hadn't called by seven, Leslie had made up her mind to make the call. She couldn't believe he didn't feel the same compatibility she did. It was two days after they'd met and still no call. Not even a call to say what a great time he'd had.

The phone ringing interrupted her anxious ruminations. "Hi, Leslie. It's Gene Lindell. Remember me?"

"Vaguely. Refresh my memory."

"I'm the guy who picked up the tab at O'Shea's a few nights ago. I'm sure you remember because you had a glass of very expensive wine."

"Now I remember. You turned pale when I ordered that glass after my second beer."

"I knew you'd remember that." They paused to let the mood shift.

"Seriously, Leslie, you probably wondered why I hadn't called sooner. I apologize and want to explain. I got caught up in some nasty trauma surgery and wasn't thinking about anything else. That's over now so I've come back to planet earth and want to see you as soon as you're available. Like, maybe tonight."

"Gene, I'd love to meet you. How about the Alhambra on Charles Street in the Village at nine?"

"You're on. And you do forgive me for the late call? Just say yes, Leslie."

"Yes, I do forgive you. And you forgive me for any not nice

thoughts I might have conjured up while waiting for that call. Okay? That's an even trade. See you in a few hours."

They waited on the street outside La Alhambra for half an hour, but the seafood paella was worth it. They emptied two flasks of Sangria that made the conversation flow even easier. The mood of two nights ago hadn't been lost.

Having gotten past the awkward getting-to-know-you stage, they were talking about their daily lives. Leslie was writing a story about police attitudes toward Blacks and how the police put stock in how young Black males dressed.

"It seems superficial but it's very real. I've talked to a large number of street cops and brass. They seem to be saying to young Blacks, 'if you dress and talk "white" you'll get a better shake from the cops.' For the Blacks it's an attack on their culture. The two groups don't seem to know how to bridge the gap. I'm going to talk to some cultural psychologists at Columbia. I find this type of work very compelling."

"I can see why, Leslie. It's real-life and you're helping to define an important issue that's at the root of our racial fissure."

"Racial fissure. I like that. May I use it without attribution?"

"It's yours Leslie. Enjoy."

Gene moved on to his own day's experience.

"I had a troubling incident in the office this afternoon. A woman came to see me about pain and instability in the area of her hip joint replacement. I operated on her just four years ago so problems with the new joint are quite premature. What bothers me is that I saw another patient a few weeks ago, after your mother, with a similar complaint. I did that hip also about four years ago. Again, quite premature. Sure, it can happen once, *maybe* twice, but three times is a serious problem."

"Sounds like the prosthesis is defective. Did they all get the same device?"

"Yes, they all got the same prosthesis, Leslie. The Arnett device. That's what's troubling me."

"Why are you troubled? I assume the device is approved by the FDA. Isn't it?"

"Sure it is. But let me tell you some more. Metro administration has been behind the Arnett device for years and strongly encourages its use by the orthopedists. It's more profitable for the hospital if we use it. So, like loyal soldiers we fell in line.

"Well, the FDA monitors surgical revisions on recently approved devices. If a device has an excessive rate of early revisions, it blows a whistle on the device. The Arnett device is over ten years in usage and has a clean track record. The monitoring period is over. The device has been given a clean bill of health."

Leslie had listened intently and already could see where Gene was heading.

"So, something has changed with the Arnett device, Gene. I don't suppose you've replaced any of the early failure prostheses? That would at least give you an opportunity to examine one."

"Well, I did one redo and managed to get the head OR nurse to let me 'borrow' the device I took out. I'm going to examine it in the pathology lab after I drop you off."

"Hey, Gene, you're not ditching this nosey reporter after telling her that intriguing story. I'm going to the lab with you."

"One last thing, Leslie. If the device has morphed into a short-lived prosthesis, many people have already received the implant, so they're ticking time bombs. Many of my patients are in that cohort. I feel guilty because I let management

steer me away from the time-tested device most orthopedists had been using when I started out in practice."

"I understand. What's done is done. Maybe the revision
rate will turn out to be less than you expect. You just have to
wait and see."

"I'm sorry I dropped this downer on our second date. We
started out so upbeat."

"Hey, Gene, as the song goes, 'into every life a little rain
must fall.' You'll weather this by doing what's right in response
to that rain."

"You're probably right, Leslie. Now let's finish this terrific
paella and get over to the pathology lab."

CHAPTER 16

The pathology laboratory was closed in the evening but Gene had borrowed a key from a friend in the department. Now he sat behind a dissecting microscope examining the hip prosthesis he had replaced earlier that very day. Leslie sat alongside him.

"It pays to have friends," he said. "The nurse in the operating room allowed me to take the prosthesis overnight. I swore to return it tomorrow so it could go to Pathology and be entered in the logbook for materials removed from patients during surgery. She knew I could be trusted. Borrowing the key to the laboratory was no problem."

Peering at the device under low magnification Gene could see small fractures on the surface of the round ball head and adjacent metal structure. The fractures would create surface friction and make it difficult for the new hip to rotate smoothly in the hip joint socket. Instability would develop since the erratic motion of the ball head would inhibit the formation of stabilizing attachment of the device to normal tissue. It was easy to see why this prosthesis had failed. The surface was defective. It was showing signs of metal fatigue. He could see it plainly. It wasn't a defect in design, it was a defect in manufacture.

"Here, Leslie. Look at this. I put the ball head under the microscope. It should be smooth. As you can see, it's pitted and full of cracks on its surface. After only four years, that's totally unexpected and unacceptable."

"As you mentioned earlier, this type of disintegration is

only showing up in more recent implants. I think the manu-facturer has to shoulder the blame along with the buyer and distributor. You're an unwitting guy in the middle, between them and the badly served patient."

"You're right on target, Leslie. The question now is why did this happen? And what is the hospital going to do about it? It's too late to spare patients who already have such devices in them. When they're informed of their predicament the lawyers will descend on Metro and AllCare."

Gene called Joel Arnett, his senior colleague who had invented the device that bore his name.

"Hi, Gene. Working a bit late, aren't you?"

"I am, Joel, and I think you'll thank me. Can you come over to the hospital now and meet me in Pathology? I know it's late, but I wouldn't have called if it wasn't important."

"I can be there in half an hour. You mean the lab on the seventh floor?"

"That's the one. I'll be waiting for you in the hallway on seven."

"Very mysterious. I'm putting on my shoes as we talk. See you shortly."

Gene met Joel Arnett in the hall, introduced Leslie, and brought him up-to-date on the story of device failure. Arnett then examined the device under the microscope.

"Why is this happening? The material is the same as on the predicate I used to get early approval. That device didn't suffer from cracks in the surface, or we would never have received a go-ahead signal from the FDA. And the lab tests we carried out never showed any breaks like these."

"This is only one prosthesis, Joel. We need to examine more devices. I had one last week and never thought to look at it this closely. That's the next step. Then we need to find out why this is happening, assuming other devices show the same fault."

Arnett looked intently at Gene. "Come to think of it, Gene, I saw an early failure in my office last week. I didn't think much of it since it seemed an isolated event but now it has me worried.

"AllCare is supplying Metro with the prostheses but what's their source? Where is that source? We're so far removed from the supplier that we take for granted that the supplier is doing careful monitoring of the manufacturing process. We should be able to take *something* for granted. Don't you think so, Gene?"

"I do, but that's why we find ourselves here in the Path Lab at ten o'clock at night. At least you can feel that your design is not the problem."

Gene paused and looked at his two companions. "I have to return this device to my friendly nurse in the OR tomorrow morning. Now I'm taking Leslie home and will try to get some sleep. It's been a long day."

"Thanks for the call, Gene. I appreciate what you did."

Gene and Leslie Ubered to her apartment house.

"I hate to end our evening on this downbeat note, Leslie. I think you understand what I'm going through."

"I do. And I commiserate with you. The evening started out great. We'll get back on track next time."

"Leslie, I know you see a good story here. I think it'll be a big one once the culprit is known."

"Trust me, I won't do anything reckless. I don't like to hurt innocent people. I know how to write stories and I know when to sit on a story. Let's talk tomorrow night."

The goodnight kiss was a friendly touching of lips. Leslie could sense the downward turn his mood had taken. It was understandable but she didn't like getting caught in Gene's darkening circumstances when she was seeking to brighten her own outlook. For the moment she'd ride the current and see where it led.

CHAPTER 17

A bright sun warmed the crisp autumn air. The Crown Bake Shop was a convenient place to meet, and Ivy and Leslie arrived almost simultaneously at noon. After a friendly greeting they set out to drop in on a couple of clothing stores they were familiar with. Each had a few favorite stores but happily was willing to go along with the other's selection. The afternoon flew by as they made a few purchases. Their tastes in clothing were different; Leslie's being traditional and Ivy's being more individual and creative. The difference made for friendly conversation and an insight into the other's personality.

"I wish I could loosen up a bit, Ivy, and venture off the beaten path into your more personal style of dress. You make clothes shopping more fun."

"Sometimes I wish I was more constrained, Leslie. My closet is full of clothes that inspired me in the store but never made it out in public."

The light banter continued into lunch. Neither was ready to open up on more guarded personal issues. That is, until Ivy volunteered that she was heading for divorce. She confessed her marriage had been moving there for several years. The conversation then grew quite personal in the area of romance and commitment. Leslie admitted her difficulty keeping her job from getting between her and romantic attachment.

The two of them felt drawn closer together by the personal nature of the conversation. When the time came to break away and head off to their respective jobs, they knew they'd begun a genuine friendship. It felt gratifying.

CHAPTER 18

The next day, Ivy again found herself doing lunch with a female, but not one she was hoping to cultivate. The lunch crowd had deserted the popular soup and salad eatery. Cheryl and Ivy pretty much had the place to themselves.

Cheryl dangled a manila envelope full of hotel and airplane receipts in front of Ivy. She showed her a few selected samples of the content. There were pictures of herself and Lester alone on a secluded beach. That set had cost her a few bucks for the hotel bellman. All in all, it was an impressive package documenting Lester's infidelity. Ivy knew Lester would not have a comparable trove of evidence regarding her time with Ted.

"Looks good, Cheryl, but what about that buried treasure map you alluded to? Is any of that financial information in this package?"

"No, that's a separate deal. This cheating stuff is just a loss leader, a freebie. I won't turn that financial stuff over until I'm sure I'm gonna get paid my share. You can understand my position. I figure the financial info is worth ten percent. You'll be getting a lead to where I think the treasure is buried. Your lawyer could take it from there."

Ivy shook her head in the affirmative. Her thoughts were contrary. *She'll never see any percent*, she thought.

"Now for the tough part, Ivy. How do I know you'll keep our bargain?"

"You don't, Cheryl. You only have my word."

"Well, that's not good enough. I've had a lawyer friend

draw up an agreement for you to sign. It stipulates a ten percent payment of your settlement. I think the terms are clear
enough. Look it over."

She handed the manilla envelope to Ivy along with a separate envelope containing the legal paper. "When you're ready
to sign we can meet and I'll pass the buried treasure info on
to you."

"I said I'd pay, Cheryl, and I will. This IOU is unnecessary.
I have no intention of going back on my word."

"It makes me more comfortable, so that's the deal."

"I'll have to think it over." With that, Ivy got up and left.

Ivy dropped off Cheryl's package at Diana's office with a
cover letter explaining what was enclosed: proof of infidelity.
She made no mention of the buried treasure.

CHAPTER 19

FedEx delivered preliminary divorce papers to Lester Brandt in his office. He was caught off guard. His PI had been unable to capture Ivy in a compromising situation with the lover Lester was sure she was bedding. He realized his position was weak since Ivy's divorce paper alleged infidelity and promised to show proof of that behavior on his part. He had no such proof to counterbalance hers. Luckily, the initial proposed settlement made no mention of his hidden assets, so he breathed a sigh of relief.

Not a good day, thought Lester. The sailing race on the river was looking better and better. That was an escape for his troubled mind but not an answer to his problems.

CHAPTER 20

Ted Swan was uneasy. He and Ivy had been avoiding the issue of their recent asexual friendship. He had no idea what had come between them. He was determined to find out tonight after the performance.

Ivy was her usual buoyant self after the standing ovation. She held Ted's hand firmly in hers as they took bows together. Afterward she told him they needed to talk. He suspected this would be the moment of truth. They didn't head to the Branville but instead took a cab uptown to a late-night diner.

"Ted, I've filed for divorce from Lester. I've been keeping us apart to avoid any situation that could weaken my case and compromise the settlement. That's the reason I've seemed so distant and kept us out of the Branville. I want to go into the divorce with clean hands and come out a wealthy woman."

"I'm glad you leveled with me, Ivy. I was afraid we were coming to the end of our run. We'll make up for lost time as soon the divorce comes through."

Ivy squeezed his hand tightly and hoped that would be signal enough to placate him. Their affair *was* over but there was no need for her to make that point at this moment.

CHAPTER 21

Cheryl sat waiting for Lester in their rendezvous apartment. She'd agreed to meet him this evening, but her heart wasn't in it. She'd turned a corner when she called Ivy and made her proposal. Lester would be kept in the dark where her deal with Ivy for his suspected cache was concerned. She knew he'd eventually figure out she'd been the source of Ivy's information regarding his hidden assets.

The divorce papers alleging infidelity surely made it clear that she had provided Ivy with *that* proof. Admittedly, infidelity in divorce cases was ubiquitous. Nevertheless, she anticipated an angry lover would soon be coming through the door.

She heard the key in the door and braced herself for Lester's entrance. To her surprise, he entered with a very ordinary expression on his face.

"I see you got my message, Cheryl, and decided to show, even after putting a torpedo into my hull. I wanted to have a few parting words with you now that we're going separate ways."

Cheryl was a bit unsure of herself as she tried to size up Lester's true intent. "I wanted to find out the terms of our parting, Lester. I wondered what you were thinking after the time we spent together. You've been very clear that marriage was not in the cards for us, so I figured you'd offer me some consolation prize."

"After you turned on me and gave Ivy that ammunition to use in court, I'm surprised you even showed up here."

"Come on, Les, I haven't injured you. Infidelity carries little weight in divorce proceedings."

His facial expression changed. It morphed into something cold and threatening.

"There is no consolation prize for backstabbing, Cheryl, so don't expect any. Just pack up your things and leave."

"Simple as all that, huh? When Ivy learns about your Cayman treasure, you'll wish you'd been more generous with the woman who shared a bed with you these past few years."

Lester saw the damage she could do if there was a fight out in the open with Ivy over his unreported income. Aside from difficulty with the IRS, kickbacks were illegal in New York State. The implications back to Eric and AllCare were considerable. He had no idea what she knew about his accumulation of payments in the Cayman bank. She obviously knew something but he didn't know if her information was potentially damaging. He decided the best course now was to placate Cheryl and put the problem in Eric's hands. It sounded as if Cheryl was yet to have the threatened conversation with Ivy.

"Maybe I was a bit harsh, Cheryl. You deserve to be treated kindlier by me. You did bend a lot to keep our affair secret. I know I was difficult on that score. Let me think about a suitable payout for you. I hate that crass term, but I'll come back to you with a generous proposal. Give me a day or two."

"Okay, Lester. Maybe we need a brief cooling off period."

Cheryl left the apartment and Lester immediately called Eric Dillon at AllCare to apprise him of the problem that loomed ahead for both of them.

CHAPTER 22

The sauna was just reaching the temperature he'd set it at when the phone rang. Eric hated to be disturbed when he was entering that magic moment; all alone with his thoughts and beginning to perspire. It was so physically perfect.

"Damn that phone," he cursed. "Eric, here. What's on your mind, Lester? I'm in the sauna so it better be good."

He listened carefully as Lester spelled out the danger he saw in Cheryl's threat to tell Ivy about the money he'd stashed away in the Caymans. Lester grew increasingly distraught as he told Eric about the meeting he'd just had with Cheryl.

"She wants recompense for our years together but I don't think that would buy us the security we need. Cheryl's a bitter woman. She's about to offer my soon-to-be-divorced wife a proposal for sharing the spoils of the divorce settlement. That would include the money I've buried in a Caribbean bank."

Eric took it all in and understood the implications.

"Okay, Lester. Keep calm. This is a serious matter. You were right to call me. Now, just listen. It's gonna be taken care of. I'll take the appropriate steps. You keep cool and in a couple of days the storm will have blown over. Stay away from Cheryl and go about your normal day's activities. Got it?"

"What are you going to do, Eric?"

"Lester, you handed the matter over to me. You're no

longer involved. End of story. Now let me enjoy my sauna." He ended the call.

An hour later, after the sauna and a shower, he felt relaxed. Lying on his bed in a terry cloth robe, he made a call to the organization's fixer. The payoff option was discussed but was deemed impermanent. He was assured the problem would be dealt with promptly at the very top level. Eric figured Cheryl had to go but he was not a party to any decision in that regard. Lester had given him Cheryl's address so he passed it on.

CHAPTER 23

Ivy grew up in rural Michigan. Her two hardworking parents treated her like a princess, and she responded by doing well in school and excelling in soccer. Her brother, four years older than Ivy, introduced her to sex in her early teens. The sex was consensual and heated; she loved her brother passionately and assumed the feeling was mutual. It wasn't. Eventually he left for college and didn't continue the physical relationship on his occasional home visits. For Ivy this was extremely painful; she saw it as the cruel desertion by a person she worshipped. A smoldering rage grew within her; anyone taking advantage of her could feel her wrath. It became a latent personality, well-concealed but ever-present. A psychiatrist might label her as having a dissociative personality disorder.

Her mother described her as "a very determined young lady" when confronted by any obstacle in her path. She was unlikely to give in to a person whom she believed was trying to exercise control over her. Ivy would put up strong resistance when confronted by such a situation. Compromise was not her usual way to solve such challenges. This characteristic made it difficult for her to form close associations.

Later that evening, after her theater performance, Ivy headed over to Cheryl's apartment. Two things were on her mind: number one, she wanted that information from Cheryl regarding Lester's hidden money, and two, she couldn't stand having Cheryl jerk her around regarding payment for the information. This was the kind of situation that brought out the physically aggressive side she usually was able to tamp down and work around. Sometimes she couldn't exercise that control.

Cheryl buzzed her in at the front door of the building and was waiting for her at the partially open door to her apartment.

"What brings you here at this hour, Ivy?"

Ivy entered the apartment. Cheryl closed the door and followed her in. Before any other words were spoken, Ivy spun around and knocked Cheryl down with a kick behind her knees. She leaped on her stunned victim, turned her on her stomach, and twisted her left arm behind her in a painful hammerlock. The martial arts course she took at the YMCA in between acting gigs was well worth the hundred fifty bucks.

"I'll get right to the point Cheryl. Don't scream for help or I'll stuff this sock in your mouth. Just listen. I want whatever information you have about Lester's hidden money. *I'm* setting the price for it. I'm tired of you dangling it in front of me and demanding a percentage of the take. There will be no negotiation. I'll pay you a flat fee, thirty thousand bucks, once I receive payment. You'll have to trust me. We don't know the size of the treasure, if there really is one. I picked an arbitrary figure to end our discussion. This is to remain strictly between us. To convince you I mean business I'm going to break your little finger before I let you up."

Ivy took the sock she'd taken from her purse, stuffed it in Cheryl's mouth, grabbed the little finger on Cheryl's left hand, hyperextended it and snapped it. Cheryl's scream was muffled. She was sobbing and shaking.

Ivy helped her get to her feet and removed the sock from her mouth.

"Now, get me that information and I'll get out of here."

A sobbing, shocked Cheryl, holding her damaged hand, went over to her desk, took a small envelope from the center drawer, and handed it to her assailant. Ivy inspected the content, gave a small smile, and headed for the door.

"You might want to visit an ER tonight to get some orthopedic attention for that finger. Sorry about your accident."

CHAPTER 24

Three days later, Connie Winter reported her daughter missing to the police. There was no evidence of foul play in Cheryl's apartment and no witnesses at work had observed anything out of the ordinary before she left for home. No one in her apartment building recalled seeing her either come home or leave her apartment that evening. That, however, was not unusual since routine coming and going was hardly noticed in the building.

CHAPTER 25

Chan Young, a NYPD homicide detective, was up for the next missing person case. Missing person cases had no obvious home so they were alternated between the Homicide and Robbery divisions.

This afternoon he was having lunch with Leslie Nugent. They were sitting in a very crowded deli on Third Avenue in the eighties eating oversized sandwiches. She enjoyed hearing about his work, and he liked to learn what she was working on. They'd met several years ago when Leslie was covering a murder story and Chan was lead detective on the case. Each had provided occasional nuggets to the other that had advanced their respective careers. Theirs was a genuine friendship and not a romance. Chan was happily married.

"So, Chan, another missing person case has come your way. How many of these actually remain forever unsolved?"

"Good question. I thought you'd ask how many of these we really ever solve. That number is more satisfying. I believe the official number is over eighty percent."

"So, you're telling me almost twenty percent of missing person cases go unsolved. What do you attribute that to? Ineptitude?" She smiled.

"I know you're kidding, Leslie. The answer is simple. No evidence. No leads. Just a stone wall."

"I'm sure there are some homicides buried in that group, Chan. Clever body disposal after an unsolved murder."

"Well, take this recent one that just fell on my plate. A

woman leaves work at Metro Hospital and is never seen again. No obvious crime to investigate. No husband. No significant other. No body. We'll look into her finances, her phone calls, question her friends, relatives and fellow workers, etc., but there's just so much time you can allocate to these cases. I agree with you that there are homicides lurking in this unsolved twenty percent but resources may be better spent elsewhere."

"Okay, Chan. I'll let you off the hook this time but I'm gonna make a file for this one and keep it on my desk. You never know. Now, what's the name of this missing woman?"

CHAPTER 26

Leslie met weekly with her editor, John Livingstone, to keep him abreast of her activities. Livingstone was in his late sixties and looked even older with a scruffy gray beard and heavily wrinkled face. He was Lincolnesque in appearance, sitting at his desk in shirtsleeves. Only the stovepipe hat was missing. The editor's office was small considering his stature at the paper. His penchant for clutter only made the space seem smaller.

Leslie cleared off the one chair for guests and sat down. The two windows behind the desk were not a distraction since John kept his shades drawn. Undrawn, the view would have been sorely compromised anyway by the absence of any outside window washer since around the time of JFK's assassination.

She told him about the failed orthopedic device and the potential for a big story. Before he could issue his anticipated note of caution, Leslie assured him she was aware that medical device failure was unfamiliar ground for her. She needed time to gain an understanding of the players and the chain of responsibility.

Livingstone heard her out and gave her a green light to see how far the story went. An actual recall would make the story more pungent. She left his office excited and eager to put a crude first draft together. Gene Lindell was involved although not guilty of any wrongdoing, but she knew he'd be tarnished by the story. This troubled her.

Back at her office, the missing person story on her desk sidetracked her for a moment. She called Chan to see if any new information had emerged.

"Very little, I'm afraid. The woman was an employee at Metro Hospital. I think I mentioned that. Name is Cheryl Winter. I think I mentioned that too. Well, she worked as an assistant to the VP for purchasing, a guy named Lester Brandt. None of her friends offered any leads to work on. One did hint that she and the VP may have been closer than just colleagues but had no real evidence of that. We're ready to drop the investigation. There are just no leads to follow."

Leslie raised an eyebrow at the mention of Metro following her conversation with Gene about the hip prosthesis problem. The missing person worked with the purchasing VP at Metro who happened to be the husband of her new-found friend, Ivy. Coincidence? Probably.

She'd put this info in the missing person file she was keeping, labeled "Cheryl Winter." You never know.

CHAPTER 27

Ten in the morning was light dozing time for Ivy. She liked to wake up slowly and adjust to the daylight hours at her own gradual pace. Her sleep mask was askew so some sunlight was finding its way to her squinting eyes. Sleep was over. She conceded that.

The telephone ring was the final announcement that day had dawned for her. She answered the phone with a still sleepy voice. She didn't even bother checking call-waiting.

"Ivy here. Who is this calling in the middle of the night?"

"Ivy, this is Kate McCallister, your hardworking agent. I have a letter in front of me from Mel Castleman. You may not know Mel. He's a director at Universal. That's Universal Studios in Hollywood. He saw you in *Climbing for Love* and wants to audition you for a part in a movie he's starting to cast. It's a serious part in a movie with Naomi Watts and Benicio del Toro. I told him you were tied up in the play and asked that he screen test you here in New York. He said he would, so I've arranged for a test tomorrow. How's that for an agent's day's work?"

"I'm wide awake now, Kate. I wasn't when you intruded on my dream state with this far-fetched story. You're a cruel person, Kate, teasing a struggling actress with a transparent fable."

"Anyway, Ivy, you be at Criterion Studios on 41st and 8th tomorrow at ten a.m. sharp. Dress casual, but nice. It won't hurt if your sexy figure is easily appreciated. I'll be there to guide you along. Don't be nervous. This could be your defining moment. See you at ten tomorrow. Ta-ta."

The line went dead.

CHAPTER 28

The lawyers for Lester and Ivy Brandt met in the conference room at Hartley and Schaefer, the office base of Ivy's attorney, Diana Gold. Glenn Morganstern represented Lester Brandt.

"Good morning, Diana. Nice to see you again."

"Same here, Glenn. Seems we did this dance not too long ago."

Each lawyer drew papers from their briefcase and spread them out on the large table in front of them.

"Okay, Glenn, let's dispense with formality and get down to business. My client, Ivy Brandt, is suing your client, Lester Brandt, for divorce. She alleges infidelity and has considerable documentation to substantiate that allegation. She's asking for half of their assets and an alimony payment of five thousand dollars a week. She's willing to forgo any claim on his retirement plan. Their apartment would be sold, and half of the net proceeds would go to my client.

"One last statement. Mrs. Brandt is an actress in the early stage of a career that has netted her a very modest income. The Brandt joint tax return lists her income last year as fifty-two thousand dollars, all derived from her acting career. That same tax return lists Lester Brandt's income from his salary and investments as six hundred seventy-six thousand dollars. That comes to around thirteen thousand dollars a week. Ivy's alimony claim seems quite reasonable in that context."

"My client will consider this claim, Diana, review the evidence supporting the alleged infidelity, and return with a counteroffer. Your cover letter implies that compiling the assets to be divided might be the most challenging issue we'll face. I'm not sure what that implies but I suspect we'll learn soon enough."

Ivy had hand delivered to Diana the information she'd gotten from Cheryl regarding the hidden assets. It strongly pointed to a bank in the Cayman Islands. That would serve as a good starting point for identifying the account or accounts they were after.

"Sounds like a start, Glenn. Let the games begin, as they say. I assume we'll hear from you in about two weeks."

CHAPTER 29

Coming out of the operating room, Gene Lindell shook his head in disappointment. His third revision operation had shown the same problem as his first. There was tissue and bone destruction with some instability of the prosthesis ball. The device wasn't forming good attachments after four years. It was easy to see why the patient had been experiencing pain and unsteadiness.

After showering and getting dressed he called Leslie and they made dinner plans. Being with her changed his mood from gloomy to elevated. She was the bright spot in his life and had come along at the time he needed a lift. Problems with the prosthesis were weighing heavy on his conscience.

Over morning coffee with Diana, Leslie lamented that her relationship with Gene was hitting a rough patch.

"He and I are good friends, Di. Trouble is, I think I'm trying to change a good friendship into a romantic relationship. It's wishful thinking on my part but I've held this hand before and I know it doesn't work out. The friendship is genuine and I don't want to lose that."

"I feel for you, Les. I really do. I understand your dilemma but it looks like you're beginning to see your way through it. Be realistic."

"I wish he wasn't caught up in this mess with the failing hip prosthesis. It's dragging him down and I can only offer solace. He feels he let his patients down and in some way he has. I don't sugarcoat it for him. I hope he can get through it, but I feel he's pushing a heavy weight up a hill. Dr. Sisyphus. My early optimism has faded.

"He was totally honest with me about his propensity to fall into what he called dark spells. He didn't want to call them bouts of depression but that's what they sound like. He admitted this might have contributed to his divorce. I worry that the hip problem is pushing him in that direction." She paused and the two fell silent.

Leslie knew she was about to blow the lid off the prosthesis story but not how it would affect Gene. It certainly wouldn't lighten his burden of guilt, and that would spill back on her and their relationship.

"Enough of that. I'm meeting him for dinner, so I have to get home and get freshened up for the evening. Seriously, though, thanks for lending a sympathetic ear."

Leslie got up to leave but abruptly sat down.

"I nearly forgot. Diana, you mentioned there was an anecdote about Ivy that you wanted to tell me. We never got to it that night at the theater. Maybe you can take a minute now to share it with me."

"Okay. Seeing that you and Ivy are becoming good friends, it may be of interest to you.

"It goes back to our time at Michigan. A sister of ours in the sorority was seriously dating a guy on the swim team. At a house party this guy met Ivy at the bar and started a conversation. She was a good listener but not at all interested in this guy whom she'd never met before. The guy's date, call her Kelly, saw them talking and watched from afar for a few minutes before interrupting what was a harmless meeting. Later that evening Kelly and her swim beau had a fight and ended their romance. Kelly blamed Ivy for the breakup, implying she had stolen her man.

"She started a rumor in the sorority that Ivy was a

predatory poacher and that women should guard their dates when Ivy was around.

"The following week a counter-rumor circulated that the poacher accusation had no foundation and should be ignored."

"That's *it*, Diana? Not a huge deal."

"Wait, let me finish. Kelly showed up before the counter-rumor appeared, with her hand in a cast. She said her little finger on one hand had been fractured in an accident."

"Are you suggesting Ivy had something to do with that injury? That she broke Kelly's finger to convince her to reverse the poacher rumor?"

"I have no evidence that's the case. I never looked into it but knowing Ivy, it isn't far-out speculation. At a reunion several years later, a friend of Kelly's hinted as much but was only offering secondhand information. That's the anecdote I wanted to tell you. And with that I have to leave and get back to my office. Diana the shark is back in the water; spouses beware."

Walking back to her apartment, Leslie mused on the anecdote Diana had related to her. There was nothing in her brief relationship with Ivy that gave credence to any violent tendency. She was a delightful companion with a normal complement of personal issues. Still, Diana felt the story was worth repeating. She hadn't let time wipe it from her memory.

CHAPTER 30

Waiting outside the office of the president of Metro Hospital, Gene Lindell was trying to keep his emotions under control. His anxiety level was near the bursting point over the impending disaster with the Arnett device. He'd made an appointment with Arnold Lasker, president of Metro, to put him on notice that the shit was about to hit the fan. Actually, the real reason was to let him know that the hospital was complicit in the Arnett device mess, and he wasn't going to let them off the hook. The administrator for surgical services had been very clear about the hospital's desire to make the Arnett device the hip prosthesis of choice at Metro. The purchasing VP had been behind the push. The Orthopedic Department had been offered sweeteners to make this happen. Implicit was the flip side of that decision. An unspoken "or else" increased the pressure to conform.

"Mr. Lasker will see you now, Dr. Lindell," was the invitation proffered by the executive secretary. Gene entered the office.

The president stood up and came around his desk to greet his visitor. Lasker was a tall man, with a clean-shaven face and neatly parted gray hair. His smile was welcoming.

"Hello, Gene. I haven't seen you in this office since we discussed the parking problem a few years ago. As I recall, that got settled to everyone's satisfaction. Have a seat and tell me what brings you here today. And please, call me Arnie."

Gene dove right in. "Arnie, I'm here to warn you about

a problem coming your way and to also let you know that I consider Metro complicit in bringing the problem about. I'm referring to a potential recall of the Arnett hip prosthesis and the patient care tragedy that device has brought about. I don't think the problem has worked its way to your office, but it will."

"You're right, Gene. This is the first I'm hearing about it."

Gene tried to maintain his composure.

"The device was given fast-track approval a number of years ago, Arnie, and signs of premature failure are only now beginning to appear."

Lasker's expression turned from warm and welcoming to deadpan serious. He sat down behind his desk and folded his hands in front of him.

"I assume we're in compliance with federal regs and have been all along. If the approval was a mistake, I don't see how that rebounds to Metro. Of course, we'll do everything we can to mitigate any damages."

"That's a good public posture, Arnie, and will save some face. I'm really here to let you know that many people have received this implant and are now ticking time bombs. They trusted us and we didn't deserve that trust. The hospital was strongly supportive of the fast-track approval. Furthermore, when that approval came through, management put pressure on the orthopedists to make the device their prosthesis of choice."

"That's hardly unusual, Gene."

"You're right, Arnie. It isn't. In this case the profit margin on each Arnett device is much greater than the margin on competitive devices. Makes it sort of a business decision." He paused to catch his breath. "Last thing I want to say. Metro does a lot of business with AllCare, the company supplying the Arnett device to us. Metro has just negotiated a better price on many of those goods AllCare sells us. I suspect the discounts are partly in exchange for the lucrative purchase of Arnett devices. Just another business decision."

"You seem to have a lot of information about our purchasing practices and have drawn some strong negative inferences about the motivation of some senior management personnel."

"I'm an unhappy physician who let my hospital's business practices invade my medical practice and keep me committed to a single hip prosthesis. I think I was left more vulnerable when a problem with the device surfaced. I'm guilty but so is Metro. Now I have to talk to Purchasing and make sure they bring in a credible alternative to the Arnett device so my orthopedic practice and that of my colleagues can continue without any prolonged interruption."

"Gene, I understand your concern. It's justified. I'm just not sure you're directing your anger at the right target. Why don't you back off a bit while I address the matter with our attorney and senior management? The first need is to bring in a new hip prosthesis so that the department's work goes on. I assume you have a device in mind to replace the Arnett. Let me fast-track *that* process."

"Okay, Arnie. I'd appreciate that. You can tell I'm all worked up over this. I dread my office hours and the specter of more patients coming in with early hip joint failure. It's depressing and embarrassing. I'll cool my jets as the kids say, but only to give you time to address the problems that are going to confront the organization."

"Thanks, Gene. Let's stay in close contact."

The two men shook hands and Gene left the office.

Lasker's next move was a call to Lester Brandt.

CHAPTER 31

The phone call from Arnie Lasker disconcerted Lester. He knew what the president wanted to talk about, face-to-face. Bad news about the Arnett hip prosthesis had finally reached the top rung of the organization. His purchasing department was largely responsible for promoting it heavily to the orthopods so he'd be drawn into any investigation, should one materialize. Dark clouds were looming on his horizon. On top of this, Ivy's divorce attorney was hinting that their asset division was more complicated than first believed.

From the smooth highway he'd been cruising on, he seemed to be detoured onto a rutted country road. It didn't feel good. Add to that Cheryl's disappearance. She'd been a pleasant diversion for him and now even that cushion was lost.

The Brandt apartment overlooked Central Park to the west. Lester and Ivy had agreed that one of them would move out temporarily while the divorce was proceeding. Ivy had moved into a small apartment, leaving Lester alone in their spacious two-bedroom residence.

He stood at the large living room window looking at the lights on the Westside buildings across the park.

The landline phone rang, and he saw an unfamiliar name on the screen.

"Hello, this is Lester Brandt. How can I help you?"

"Hi, Mr. Brandt, I'm Leslie Nugent. We met briefly at the

Metro gala. I was with Len Walling. We were talking to your wife. I'm the reporter with *the Times*."

"You're slowly creeping back into my memory, Ms. Nugent. A young blond woman in a black cocktail dress, if I recall."

"You have a very good memory, Mr. Brandt."

"Okay, let's dispense with the formality. I'm Lester and you're Leslie. Now, what's on your mind?"

"Okay. I'm writing a piece about the process that new medical devices go through before being approved for use in patients. I've read a bit about the FDA approval process and feel it would be helpful if I could talk to someone in a hospital who has to assess a new device before deciding to purchase one. I don't have to cite you by name in my article."

Lester now had a clearer picture of the woman he was speaking to. He'd had trouble taking his eyes off her at the gala.

"Well, we can talk about the attribution after the interview. This is Tuesday evening. Why don't we meet at the Eclipse Bar on Third Avenue, tomorrow at this time? The bar is between East 83rd Street and 84th. Is that okay?"

"Better than okay, Lester. I'll see you tomorrow evening. Good-bye."

He sat back and reflected. He was no fool. The reporter obviously had gotten wind of the hip joint problem and was seeking an audience with him on the weak pretext of understanding the hospital approval process with regard to new medical equipment.

Leslie put down her phone. Her primary objective was to learn what role the hospital played in the hip prosthesis misfortune. This was an open-ended inquiry to acquire basic information in an area where she was a novice. Lurking in the background, however, was her curiosity about what role he had, if any, in the missing person case she and Chan had discussed. The missing woman, after all, was his assistant. The police might be ready to drop the case but she wasn't so inclined until she spoke with Lester Brandt.

She'd failed to mention either item on her agenda and hoped she could somehow work around to the real reasons for the interview.

CHAPTER 32

Wednesday evening Leslie cabbed over to the Eclipse. She found Lester seated at a corner table with a half-finished drink in front of him. He rose with a warm smile and welcomed her with a handshake.

"Name your drink, Leslie. I'm having a single malt on the rocks."

"Sounds good to me."

He stood up, walked over to the bar, and came back with two drinks. "Tell me a little about yourself, Leslie."

"I'll make it brief. A Long Island girl finishes college and finds a reporter job in D.C. on a small Virginia daily. After twelve years she scores a big story and is recruited to *the Times*. She meets an orthopedic surgeon, learns that there might be a problem with hip devices he implants in people. She begins to piece together a story starting with the FDA device approval process." She ended with a smile.

"Terse and to the point, Leslie." Lester smiled inwardly. He knew the hip joint problem was on her agenda.

Over the next half hour they talked about the approval process. Leslie had a fairly good understanding of it from her reading and from Gene's critical evaluation of the way approval came about. She was impressed with the depth of Lester's knowledge about the process.

"Are you aware of any difficulties with hip joint prostheses at Metro?"

Lester chose to play dumb. He didn't know how much she

knew, but he thought it best to stay away from the subject with a reporter.

"That's news to me but I'll certainly look into it. Purchasing only buys the devices the doctors ask for. We don't question their judgment."

Leslie could see this was not going to be a productive area to pursue with him and decided to drop it.

"How about a refill, Leslie? I think we've exhausted this subject."

"Sure. I'm up for a second of what must be very expensive scotch."

Lester steered the conversation in a more personal direction. Leslie was uneasy with this course correction. It was not within her reporter's range of interest.

"Ivy would be coming on stage right about now. Have you seen the play?"

"Of course, Lester. She's terrific. The play is quite good, but she takes it into the realm of big hits. I don't know how it will fare if she leaves it."

"Someone else's problem, fortunately. I bet she's being looked over for other acting roles. We don't talk a lot lately. Our hours are a poor match."

Leslie saw an opening here to get into matters more private but had to let him lead there. He seemed very different from the confident man she'd met at the gala.

"Do you care to talk about it, Lester? You hardly know me but I'm a very good listener."

He appeared to welcome her invitation. Leslie thought he was mildly depressed.

"Our marriage has been on weak legs for many years but was never bad enough to talk divorce. Are you married, Leslie?"

"No, I'm not and never have been."

"Don't know how you've managed to stay free. Can't imagine you staying single for so long. Am I being too intrusive, Leslie? You probably have a longtime live-in. Is that it?"

"Again, I plead not guilty. No live-ins, no husbands. Not even a cat."

"Unbelievable."

"You know, being single isn't so bad when compared with living in a strained marriage, Lester. I've never experienced the latter, but I don't think I'd tolerate it very well."

"Having a life outside the marriage is one way to compensate for the absence of life within the marriage. You know, Leslie, many affairs are a perfectly understandable response along the pathway to divorce. An affair shouldn't necessarily be thought of as something immoral."

Leslie found herself getting too deep into Brandt's personal life. That hadn't been her objective, but it did raise an interesting road to follow. She decided to push it a bit.

"I wasn't being judgmental, Lester. It's also a fact of life, working in a setting heavily populated by women, like a hospital. But while we're being intrusive, I read in the paper that a woman in your department disappeared last week."

"Hold it right there, Leslie. I can see where you're going. Cheryl and I were good friends and I miss her. I visited her mother and tried to comfort her. The police came by the office and questioned me and some of the staff in the office. We were all completely surprised by her disappearance, none more so than me. I'm baffled by it. I'd be the last guy to want Cheryl to disappear."

Leslie was surprised by the emotional nature of his response. It seemed a bit strong for his office relationship with the missing woman. But she thought this was about as far as she could go. She barely knew him, but his genuine sadness had gotten to her. She thought it best to leave.

"Lester, this has been a productive evening. I think it's time for me to go."

He walked her out to the street.

"It was very kind of you to give me so much of your time, Lester. I mean it."

They shook hands and he hailed her a cab.

She called Chan when she got home and told him about her visit.

"He's not the guy, Chan. I think he's genuinely upset about his missing assistant. He denied anything more than friend-ship, but I wasn't completely sold. He didn't have a role in her disappearance, Chan. I'm reasonably sure of *that*."

"Okay. That's helpful but doesn't get us closer to solving the missing person case. We'll keep looking, but where?"

"He also admitted his marriage was on the rocks and a divorce was being considered. I already knew that from a conversation with his wife. Lots of gloom hanging over the guy."

"Hey Les, sounds like you did more than conduct an interview for a story. I mean it. You should hear yourself."

"Okay. I admit I was a bit taken with the guy, but nothing happened, Dad. You can relax; I'm still the same gal you met with yesterday. Have a good night, Chan."

CHAPTER 33

The studio was a bare-bones setup with several rooms equipped with all manner of recording equipment and lighting. Ivy sat in a room with cameras and voice recording equipment. She studied a script, preparing herself to read her lines on cue and offer the appropriate facial expressions as indicated in the script.

Kate McCallister, seated nearby, chatted with Desmond Walcott, casting director for this film. The room was relatively quiet considering how many people were deep in conversation.

"Listen up, everyone. We're going serious now. All conversation should stop or be taken outside. I'm Desmond Walcott and I'm in charge of the test we're going to be running. I want to run it once, then coach the actor for specific nuances and see if the second run-through will suffice. Ivy, just focus on the script and me. I'll be acting the part opposite you. Okay? I assume that head nod was an affirmative. Lights, camera, action."

The test ran without a break. Ivy performed as if she'd done this a hundred times. The second run-through sufficed. When it was over, Walcott told her what a professional job she'd done. For a first-timer, he said, a double take was a miracle. Now they'd review the video together and see how it looked.

An hour later Walcott was ecstatic. "Great. And I mean it. Ivy, we're done here. You couldn't have done any better.

Next, you'll have an interview with Jack Bauman, the executive producer of the movie."

"What's he like, Desmond?"

The testing director hesitated. He looked up to the sky before answering.

"Hard to say. He's very experienced in producing movies and always interviews the major players. He's rejected some very good actors and actresses, but his judgment must be sound because his pictures *always* make money. Just be yourself. You'll do fine."

"Thanks, Desmond. I hope we get to work together."

Kate hugged Ivy, who was grinning ear to ear.

"I think you're in, Ivy. I'm thinking this will be the beginning of something exciting."

"It felt so natural, Kate. I didn't know what to expect but it turned out to be a pleasant day's work. I loved it. I guess they'll call to schedule an interview with Jack Bauman. Seems he has the last word."

"After that we go over the contract and hopefully sign on. Considering Desmond's enthusiastic reaction, I bet we can negotiate more money and a few perks. But let's see the initial offer first. The key here is to not seem greedy. If they find you easy to work with, I'm sure there'll be more work down the road."

Ivy left the studio on a real high.

Kate called Ivy later that day and told her the interview was scheduled for the next afternoon at five in Bauman's suite in the Baronet Hotel. She told her to go to the eighteenth floor and find room 1807.

Bauman greeted her at the door and welcomed her in. Jack Bauman, a slightly overweight man in his mid-fifties she guessed, had a ruddy, clean-shaven face and receding hairline. His welcoming smile was engaging and displayed a sparkling set of teeth. He was wearing a black workout suit, a T-shirt and sweatpants, with house slippers. Ivy was dressed casually, as she was told, in a skirt and sweater.

She accepted his offer of a glass of white wine. He was also drinking white wine.

"Nice of you to come, Ivy. I've seen the screen test and think you have the look I'm after. The acting was fine as well."

"I'm so glad you were pleased, Mr. Bauman. Desmond ran a tight ship. He's a pleasure to work for."

"I guess you know, Ivy, that the part is just a step below a lead role. The character is a woman trying to seduce a wealthy businessman. She gains entry to his world by becoming the close friend of his daughter. I'd like to see you in that role. It does call for some nude scenes as she finds her way into his bed. We have doubles, of course, for the more explicit takes.

"Since that's a central part of the role I'd like to see you with less clothing on. Why don't you step into the bedroom next door and slip into the negligee on the hanger? It's similar to the one you'd wear in the bedroom scene."

Ivy went into the room and found the negligee lying on the bed. Her mind was clear and in focus. She was no struggling ingénue ready to screw a producer for any part in a major motion picture. On the other hand, she wanted this part, badly, and might be willing to use her sexuality to guarantee her spot in the production. She'd give him what she was sure he wanted, only in exchange for what *she* wanted. As a trade it didn't sound so seamy. And he wasn't a creepy old man. He was a nice-looking guy.

She came out of the bedroom in the negligee and the silk slippers that had been left on the bed beside it. Jack was standing next to the bar. He put down his glass and walked toward her.

"I knew you'd pass the negligee test. Never had a doubt."

He moved to put an arm around her waist. She let him, but she leaned back, turned away and didn't allow him to kiss her. She could tell he was aroused.

"Is this part of the 'negligee test,' Jack? I don't think you need to get up close and personal to judge my suitability for the role."

"Ivy, I think you pass the test with flying colors. This is just a way you can show your appreciation."

"I understand, Jack. And once there's a signed contract in my hands, I'll be sure to thank you for its generous terms in a manner that would please you. In the meantime, I have to get dressed and move on to my next appointment."

She spun out of his grasp and slowly walked back to the bedroom. His eyes were on her all the way to the bedroom until the door closed behind her. He'd considered making a heavy-handed move on her to get what he wanted, but something in her manner made him hold back.

The final contract called for $30,000 a week with a guarantee of $500,000. The picture was scheduled to begin shooting in one month and to take an estimated four months. Kate thought this was a very good year's pay for a first film.

Ivy visited Jack Bauman in his suite before he left for Hollywood. She expressed her thanks in more ways than he expected.

CHAPTER 34

Ivy was thinking about her divorce. It appeared that the big payout she had been so obsessed with might be eclipsed by her own new earning potential. That gave her pause to reconsider her strategy.

In a recent conversation with Leslie, she'd learned that Cheryl Winter had disappeared only a day or so after she'd turned over the information about Lester's hidden assets to her attorney. She recalled going over to Cheryl's apartment that evening but had only a faint recollection of their interaction. Her attorney was bound to ask how she'd accumulated the evidence. If she admitted that Cheryl had provided it, the next logical question would be why she'd done that. Other questions would follow. The question of Cheryl's motive and Ivy's dealings with her could be a problem. Cheryl's disappearance bothered her. She realized that the package of evidence documenting Lester's infidelity was her only link to Cheryl.

Ivy decided to get the evidence packet back and just sue for divorce without Cheryl's hard proof of Lester's infidelity. The hidden assets could be negotiated last. Her world looked different now with her movie contract in hand.

She dialed her lawyer's office. "Ivy Brandt for Diana Gold."

After a pause, Diana was connected. "Hello, Ivy. Nice to hear from you. There's no news for you on this end. Is there something new you wanted to tell me?"

"Yes, Diana. Maybe we can do it over the phone. My

situation is changing. I've been offered a serious part in a movie, and it changes my financial outlook considerably. I'd like to proceed with the divorce but without the heavy emphasis on infidelity. I know you think the case for that is pretty strong, based on the evidence I provided. That's the next thing. I want to take back that packet of evidence. I can't tell you why but that's my wish. You can scale back the claim on Lester if that's indicated. I suspect it might be."

"I understand, Ivy. I'm curious why you're retreating but something tells me you're not going to offer an explanation. I won't badger you with questions, I'll just FedEx the package to you and email you a revised claim on your husband. After you read it, we should meet down here to discuss our new strategy. Call my office for an appointment when you're ready."

"Thanks for being so patient with me, Diana. You can be sure I gave this serious thought before calling you. I'll be in touch once I receive your email. One last thing, don't FedEx the package to me. I'd rather pick it up myself at your office. Thanks."

Ivy breathed a sigh of relief. A near stumble was averted.

Diana turned her chair around and stared out the office window. She ran a series of scenarios through her mind to understand what had happened to make Ivy undermine her own winning case. Surely she wasn't going soft on her husband. All the discussions they'd had made it clear that she harbored no affection for him. Did she fear retribution from him? Unlikely, if she was being truthful about her own infidelity. Did a "messy" divorce threaten her new movie career? Could be, but this wasn't going to be very messy. Plus, the mess was on her husband's side. No, none of those scenarios seemed to work.

She got up and poured herself a scotch on the rocks. Back

in her chair she continued to stretch her imagination. Maybe there was something in or about the actual evidence that she didn't want to put on display. She'd gone over the evidence herself and saw a pretty good record of deceit. Come to think of it, how did she get all that evidence? Even a private eye would have had difficulty coming up with such a good record. So, who could collect so much paper? Her husband was not likely to be the source of his own destruction...

Whoa.

The only other person who could have gathered such a trail of infidelity was the other woman. Of course. In all her divorce cases she never had seen one in which the third party ratted out the husband to the wife. Toward what end? The usual reason. Money. Lester's lover sold him out. Okay. But why would Ivy now drop that part of the case? She had no good explanation, and her next client was in the waiting area.

CHAPTER 35

The cast party for Ivy was bittersweet since the production was losing its leading lady, but the fact that she was headed to the big time reflected positively on the play. The party was being held in the back room of Zavara's, a Greek restaurant in the Village. Leslie and Diana were invited and cabbed over separately. Once inside the restaurant, Leslie saw that she recognized no one. Was this the wrong night? Diana arrived shortly after, on her way home from work. She happily found a familiar face and soon she and Leslie were doing small talk until they were ready to take on the theater crowd. Well, maybe after a drink or two.

"I'm not trolling for a story this evening, Diana. It's very unusual for a reporter to take down her antenna and just enjoy the free alcohol."

"I wish I could shut down my mind for an evening, Leslie. Something's always cooking on my stove, even if it's just simmering."

"Okay, Diana, what's burning your brain cells at this very moment? Maybe I can help. Give me a shot."

"Try this one on for size, 'Miss Reporter on Break'. I see all kinds of divorces. I have one where the wife has a winning case alleging infidelity and chooses, at the last minute, to withdraw the very convincing evidence and even accept a reduced settlement. I haven't been able to figure this one out!"

"Let me give it a try, Di."

"I'm all ears."

"So, the wife is afraid of her own evidence. Maybe it contains incriminating stuff that works against her. A double-edged sword, so to speak. She fears what it says about her isn't worth the settlement she'd reap. So why did she start down this road with this evidence in the first place? That's too simple. She'd have purged the bad stuff. Still could, but doesn't seem so inclined. I don't like this scenario."

"I agree, Leslie. Try again."

"Diana, where did the evidence come from?"

"Not specified."

"That sounds a bit unusual. Maybe a spiteful mistress. I guess that's it. But that doesn't explain the wife's reticence to use it to her advantage. Maybe the price was too high. Well, she has the evidence so she must have agreed to pay the price. Or did she? Wait a minute. Spiteful mistress is asking too much, so wife agrees to pay but gets rid of mistress and doesn't have to pay. So why withdraw the evidence? That was the question, wasn't it? Because the evidence links her to the mistress who has been eliminated. That's it. The evidence links the wife to the now deceased mistress."

"I hate to admit it, Les, but that's a damn good postulate."

"Thanks, Diana. That's the reporter in me sniffing out the story. Now tell me if it matches the facts you have."

"I'm afraid it does. Up until the murder, that is. I owe you, Leslie. You have to promise me this conversation stays between us and us alone." Leslie nodded. "The wife in the case is your new friend, Ivy Brandt. She's my client. She picked up the evidence pack personally and has directed me to reduce the claim we made."

Leslie froze.

"Diana, step outside with me so I can tell you something

chilling. I don't want our conversation to be overheard by anyone in this room."

They worked their way through the crowd and finally were out in the fresh air.

"Wow, Leslie. Are we playing out a Hitchcock scene? What's so secret?"

"I guess each of us has been playing with half a deck, Diana. Now we put our cards together and see a full one."

"Enough with the metaphor, Leslie. Out with it."

"The woman who may have been Lester Brandt's mistress is missing. The police don't have a clue what happened to her, and they have tried. Plug her into my convoluted story and you take it from there. Ivy didn't want to have to explain to anyone, especially you, where the evidence came from. It links her directly to the missing mistress. Ergo, she removes the evidence, reduces her claim, and launches a lucrative movie career, which obviates the need for a more generous settlement."

"Now I understand why the evidence is out."

"And we can theorize what happened to the missing mistress. Or at least the *presumed* mistress...presumed by me. It's all just conjecture, nothing more. Hey, aren't you glad you stopped in on this party on your way home, Diana?"

Leslie eventually got to congratulate the guest of honor.

"I saw you and my lawyer huddling in a very conspiratorial manner, Leslie. I hope I wasn't the subject of your confab. It looked very intense, I must say."

"Never you worry, Ivy. Your star is on the rise so all you have to do is sit back and enjoy the ride. Diana and I are mere mortals on this planet. All we can do is watch with wonder."

"Thanks for those elegant words. I hope my scriptwriter hands me simpler stuff, Leslie."

"Well, good luck, Ivy." They hugged warmly and parted smiling.

Leslie called Chan and made an appointment to meet at their favorite lunch hangout in two days. She told him she had breaking news of considerable interest.

CHAPTER 36

A lot was going on in Lester's life. His attorney had called with the good news that Ivy had withdrawn her scorched earth demands and would now agree to a simple divorce with the condo shared fifty-fifty and alimony payment of $4,500 a week. She'd withdrawn her claim of infidelity without giving any reason. It was a good deal, and he took it. The only remaining piece was the asset division. For some reason, that remained to be settled. Lester couldn't imagine that Ivy had gotten a handle on his offshore assets.

The Arnett device was a separate problem. Device failure was going to sink it. Only question was whether it would take him down with it.

Sitting in his newly rented apartment watching the sunset, scotch in hand, he was brooding about the turn his golden life had taken. Ivy was walking away with a good settlement right into a lucrative new career. He wondered why she'd eased up on the settlement, but he gave it very little thought.

CHAPTER 37

Chan and Leslie stopped at a lunch cart on the walkway just outside Central Park. They carried their falafel rollups to a bench inside the park. Leslie was eager to try out her theory of Ivy's crime on Chan. While they devoured their lunches, she went through her conversation with Diana Gold. It made sense once you tied together Ivy's withdrawal of the evidence she had on her husband and the disappearance of the presumed mistress.

"Pretty good work, Leslie. Want to come and work in our homicide division? I like your story. Trouble is we have no body, so we have no crime to investigate. Sometimes we can proceed without a body but the circumstantial evidence in this case is not as compelling as one would like. To make the reasonable inference of murder here is one thing. There's no evidence to pin it on Ivy Brandt. It's plausible but not compelling. Sorry to sound so professorial. I think you've got us pointed in the right direction. And that's critical. Now we need to strengthen the argument."

"I appreciate your assessment, Chan. I was so overwhelmed by the eureka moment that I didn't give the evidence a really hard look. Where do you think we need to go next?"

"Now we have a theory of the disappearance. At least that gets us off the dime. A conversation with Ivy Brandt might be interesting. Trouble is the info about her divorce was given to you in confidence by her attorney, a good friend of yours.

It could cost you a friend and injure her attorney-client relationship. I'm going to leave this in your hands to sort out. I also think that Ivy Brandt's motive for murder seems thin, at best. Go easy, Leslie."

"Good advice, Chan. Thanks for the words of caution. You were right, as usual. Talk to you soon."

CHAPTER 38

AllCare had offices in New York City and White Plains, New York. Eric Dillon, AllCare's president, sat back in a comfortable leather chair in his Manhattan office. He'd taken his in-law's wedding gift and expanded it into a giant medical supply company doing over $6 billion a year in imports and domestic products.

The Arnett device was just one of a multitude of products he brought into the States. He relied on dozens of factories in China, Sri Lanka, and Vietnam for those products.

Lester Brandt was on the speakerphone.

"Just giving you a heads-up, Eric. It looks like the Arnett device may be experiencing premature failure problems. I don't have any details yet, but I'd certainly trace the device back to its source. Call this friendly advice."

"Mighty friendly gesture, Les. Keep me posted on any further developments with the device. Maybe it'll just turn out to be a small glitch. Keep your fingers crossed. Let's meet for lunch sometime this week. My secretary will set us up."

Eric was left wondering after the call ended. The device Arnett had submitted to the FDA over ten years ago mimicked the popular Altschuler device in every important aspect. The particular sample device fully lived up to the specs they'd submitted. Altschuler was a perfect predicate to base the review on. Eric had personally helped Joel Arnett through the review process in exchange for advanced standing in the soon-to-be-completed buyout process. Now Lester had warned him off the pending buyout proposal. He was left to wonder where the train had left the track.

Leslie Nugent, expecting a dour Gene Lindell to meet her for dinner, found herself instead confronted by an energetic, talkative guy. Instead of his recent woe-is-me self he was anxious to tell her about his discovery.

"I know I've been in a funk lately over the hip device problem, Les, but last night I came out of it. I feel better even though the problem persists. The difference is that the device failure is not due to a fault in Joel's design but rather in some manufacturing error. For some reason I feel less derelict in my responsibility."

"Wait a minute, Gene. Back up a bit and give it to me slowly."

"Okay. You remember we examined an Arnett device under a microscope. It was one I had very recently replaced. It showed unusual cracking in the protective covering of the device's ball. It wasn't a design failure. This was a failure in the manufacturing process that had occurred within the past four or five years. Switching to the Arnett device may have been a reasonable move years before. It was undermined years later by something not in the design of the device."

Leslie felt that Gene was rationalizing away his guilt. She could understand his reasoning, subtle though his logic was. She was glad to see him sweep away the funk he'd been living in. But, switching to her reporter mode, she had the scent of a story here.

"Where is the device manufactured, Gene? And who is responsible for the quality of the product?"

"I'm sure it's made somewhere in Asia. I guess the manufacturer shares a large portion of the responsibility for the product with the actual supplier in the States. Wait a second. The device comes to us in a box which I've seen in the OR supply room and I believe the country of origin is Vietnam. The supplier, of course, is AllCare. Metro does a lot of business with AllCare. Why are you asking these questions?"

"Didn't the FDA approve this device based on its similarity to one it approved several years before? I think they call it a predicate."

"I believe so, Leslie. But, so what?"

"Well, I assume the predicate never showed similar cracks in its protective covering. I'm also assuming the protective covering was the same in order for the predicate concept to be valid. So, here's my reporter's nose catching a foul scent. Remember Volkswagen's fake data on their diesel cars? Apply that here. The FDA is given a device that matches the predicate in all aspects it called for. Then, many years later, after final approval is given, devices begin to fail prematurely. Was this due to an innocent error or is something devious involved? If it was a greedy move to cut costs in the manufacturing process, for example, the manufacturer had to believe the less costly devices were good enough and wouldn't fail. Bad judgment by greedy people and now patients are paying the price."

"Leslie, I admire your ability to see through the fog and find the enemy. I mean it. You have an uncanny sense of reasoning, and it usually is right on the money. But now let's get on with ordering the meal we came here to enjoy."

Leslie found Gene's lighter mood unsettling. His patients were still stuck with defective hips regardless of the reason for the premature device failure. He never *was* a culprit in the sorry fiasco. She didn't see how he was off the hook he never had been on and how this served to so visibly brighten his mood. She was troubled by his behavior.

Gene seemed to be putting the Arnett tragedy behind him before it had fully evolved. His seeming disinterest in any aspect of the misfortune was off-putting for her. She wondered if she'd misjudged him. Or if he was manifesting subtle signs of bipolar disorder. That was a far reach, but his behavior was disquieting.

Later that evening, sitting on her bed, Leslie could see that the point of manufacture needed to be examined. And examined by someone who didn't have a financial stake in the outcome of the exam. This set her to wondering about the financial stake. Who were the stakeholders in this game?

In her methodical and calculating manner, she envisioned the steps she needed to take to dissect this story. She'd visit the factory in Vietnam and meet the person supervising manufacture of the device. She'd determine if the manufacturing process had changed and, if so, what the change was. And why had it been necessary? If she got that far she'd know if there was a big story to be pieced together or just some innocent mistake in production that didn't demand a lot of her attention, in spite of the human cost.

CHAPTER 39

Banks in the Cayman Islands touted themselves as the Swiss banks of the Caribbean; same privacy without the snow. They were very secure and resistant to any snooping into personal accounts. There was one difference they didn't advertise: with the right amount of cash an interested party could find a friendly banker willing to reveal some useful information about an account. Such behavior was very unlike what one would encounter in Switzerland.

Diana Gold reviewed the very limited information her investigator had been able to shake free from a bank vice president at Cayman International. The bank VP said the account itself was untouchable but all Diana wanted to know was if Lester Brandt had an account at Cayman and what the balance was. Those two pieces of information had cost her client $10,000. Ivy had gambled and the gamble paid off. Lester had an account with over $9 million.

Diana met with Glenn Morganstern in his office without the adversarial couple.

"I assume you have some updated information about the assets we're trying to allocate, Diana. From the pleased expression on your face, I don't think the news is favorable for my client."

"Depends how you look at it, Glenn. He may have to give up something, but this may allow us to close the book on the divorce."

"Okay, Diana. What have you got?"

"I've got a Cayman bank account with over nine million squirreled away. Nothing unusual about a husband keeping assets out of his wife's field of vision. One caveat is that there's no way he could have amassed this small fortune given his salary and their expenses. I'm not going to pursue that in these proceedings, but it does suggest that Lester Brandt has an income stream he's not sharing with *anyone*, including, probably, the IRS.

"My proposal is that our two parties quietly divide his hidden assets and then just walk away. I haven't discussed any of this with my client. Rather than let her smell blood I'd like to have a settlement in hand when I go talk to her."

"I tend to agree with you, Diana. Best if both parties feel they're coming out winners. Why not leave Lester with sixty percent of the Cayman money? That might give him some small satisfaction."

"Let's settle at a fifty-five-forty-five split, and you buy me lunch, Glenn."

"Works for me, Diana."

CHAPTER 40

New York to Hanoi was an overnight adventure with a stopover in Los Angeles. Leslie's editor approved the trip and even got accounting to spring for business class all the way. Not too shabby, she thought.

At Noi Bai International Airport, she was met by a young *Times* representative who escorted her through customs and by cab to her hotel in downtown Hanoi. She indicated that she would accompany Leslie tomorrow on her trip to meet with Tuan Banh at his factory just thirty minutes outside the city. Tonight, Leslie could use the time to catch up on her sleep. The woman, Victoria Nguyen, was Vietnamese and spoke perfect English. When Victoria suggested they have dinner together, Leslie welcomed the opportunity to acquaint herself with some local customs.

Dinner at a restaurant chosen by Victoria offered the best of Vietnamese cuisine. Leslie found a number of shrimp dishes that sounded tantalizing. Victoria helped her pick out one they could share. They ordered a bottle of wine and dug into the hors d'oeuvres.

"Victoria, do you know why I'm here? It might help tomorrow if you did."

"Leslie, I wasn't given any information about the reason for your trip."

Leslie proceeded to lay out her concerns about the manufacture of the hip device.

"I need to know if I'm getting honest answers to my

questions or if Tuan is afraid to reveal any actions he may have taken that will compromise his standing with his American customers. You can help me read his responses."

"I think you have to accept what he's willing to reveal. Caution will characterize his answers. From what you told me he may be responsible for some ill-advised changes in the manufacturing process. I don't think he'll jeopardize his contract. He has a lot at stake, so you need to give him wiggle room."

"Thanks, Victoria. I have no intention to come on too strong and be accusatorial. If you think I am, let me know."

The factory was in two parts: an older section composed of cement block walls with a corrugated metal roof, and a newer wooden section twice the size of the old, original portion. The workforce consisted mostly of women seated on backless benches with a mix of devices in various stages of completion on the long table in front of them. Leslie recognized several hip prostheses on the table.

A slim Vietnamese man in an open collar white shirt and navy trousers introduced himself to Leslie and Victoria.

"Welcome to my factory. I am Tuan Banh. I was expecting you two ladies."

He extended his hand to Leslie. She reached out and shook it.

"You must be Leslie Nugent from the US and *the New York Times*, and your guide must be Victoria Nguyen. Let me show you around the factory, then we can have some tea and discuss the reason why you made such a long trip to see me."

They toured the facility with Tuan carefully pointing out items of interest. The tour lasted about an hour and ended in Tuan's office where a young woman served them tea and pastries.

"Okay, Ms. Nugent. I'm at your service."

"Thank you for the tour, Mr. Banh. It was instructive. I won't take up too much of your time. My interest is in the Arnett hip device. I don't know if you're aware that there have been some premature failures of the device. I'd like to know if any change has taken place in its manufacture over the past four years. Let's start there."

"You may be aware, Ms. Nugent, that the profit margin on devices made for sale to US companies is quite small. We are under intense pressure when contracts are up for renegotiation. The buyer always, and I do mean *always*, seeks a lower price. Buyers seem to think that there is no bottom price; that we can always go lower. Naturally, the only way we can survive is to lower *our* cost and one way we lower our cost is to look for less expensive providers of the materials we use to make the product. Am I making myself clear?"

"I'm following, Mr. Banh. Why don't you just continue."

"Four years ago, I changed my supplier for the cobalt chromium alloy, the principal metal in the hip prosthesis. My previous supplier was very reputable, but his price left me no choice. I had to search the market for an alternative supplier who was less expensive. I am aware of the American saying, 'you get what you pay for.' I had no choice. I needed to cut my cost to survive. I hoped the less expensive alloy would work just as well. Now you tell me that may not have been the case."

"I'm afraid that *is* the case. It may be a situation where the greed of your buyer forced you into a compromised situation and he ended up unwittingly buying an unsatisfactory product."

The three sat silent for a minute.

"Tuan, did you tell your buyer about the change in your supplier?"

"There was no need to since the materials were the same

as far as anyone knew. Still, I felt uncomfortable. The new supplier of the alloy did not have the same reputation for quality as the original provider. The contract didn't ask for the names of suppliers of different materials used in the manufacture. Nevertheless, I told the buyer about the change. I did it to protect myself if anything went wrong. It was a cowardly thing to do since I knew he was not likely to pursue the matter."

Leslie could see why the problem had surfaced—neither the manufacturer nor the buyer took the pains to assess the quality of the modified device before implanting it in patients.

"I appreciate your honesty in answering my questions. Just a few more questions. How much are you paid for each device, Tuan?"

"One thousand six hundred and fifty dollars. We were paid three hundred more per device under the old contract. That's a big difference for me to absorb. I had to reduce my cost."

"Last question. Can *you* see any difference in the alloy you're using now compared to the one in the previous contract?"

Tuan hesitated and then chose his words carefully. "I think I've helped you all I can Ms. Nugent. I have to get back to work now."

With that, Tuan Banh stood up, bowed gracefully to his guests, and left the room. Victoria indicated to Leslie that the meeting was over.

"I think Mr. Banh has said all he's going to on this subject. He's embarrassed."

"Thank you, Victoria. We can head back."

CHAPTER 41

Filming was an exciting experience for Ivy. It was so different from the theater. Pieces of the story were shot out of sequence. The final film was what mattered. The actors often ignored the previews and some never even watched the final product. Not Ivy. She was very into her part and, like the other cast members, had a good understanding of the part and its meaning in the bigger story. She relished seeing the previews and most certainly looked forward to the final film.

Shooting took place in New York City, so her life was minimally impacted.

Now, nearly halfway through the shoot, her only concern was that she had no gig lined up following this one. Her salary checks arrived on time and gave her some cheer.

Her divorce finally came through. The final settlement of assets had been a minor skirmish. The size of Lester's hidden stash was a stunner. Cheryl had been insightful. A Cayman bank VP, Mason Lord, came at a cost but his information proved worth it. Ivy had resisted the fifty-five-forty-five split at first but could see Lester was dug in. Rather than prolong the agony, she acquiesced. Her bank account swelled by nearly $4 million, giving her a nice cushion if there was a long break before her next part.

One loose end bothered her. When she got the package of evidence back from Diana, she thought that was the end of it.

Her mistake. Lester had to wonder how she knew about the money hidden in the Caymans. He wasn't stupid. He must have surmised that Cheryl had been the source of the information. She was the only one who *might* have known. Did that connect to her disappearance? There was no way to tell. And so what? She laughed.

CHAPTER 42

Keeping Jack Bauman content wasn't as unpleasant as she'd imagined at the outset. The sex was average for her but Jack was more than satisfied. She saw him once or twice a month, depending on when he was in town. Fortunately for her, he spent a lot of time on the West Coast. What bothered her was knowing that she was dependent on Jack.

She couldn't afford to break away from him. Her movie future was in his hands, and she hated *that* the way she disliked the thought of sharing her divorce settlement with Cheryl.

Ivy was fast losing patience with Jack Bauman. She intended to find out if he had a future part for her when the current picture was completed. The director estimated they were four weeks from the end of the shoot. She and Jack were meeting in his hotel suite that evening for dinner.

Ivy arrived at the suite on time, wearing the kind of slinky dress he enjoyed seeing her in. Jack was in his usual loungewear outfit, lightweight sweatpants and matching zipper-front jacket. Over dinner she raised the issue of a role to follow the one she was now finishing.

"Jack, I was wondering if you had a role for me when my current shoot ends. I've been given to understand that we have about a month to go."

"Well, no, I don't have anything in the works right now. But what's the problem? A small hiatus between pictures shouldn't bother you."

"I guess that depends on how long the hiatus is. You know how long it takes to read a script, do any rewrites, carry out testing and casting, obtain sets and assemble a work crew. If that has to start from scratch it could be many months before the actors are finally brought on. I'm looking for work and a paycheck starting no more than a few months after this current gig ends. If the role is smaller than my current part and the pay commensurately smaller, a long hiatus may not work for me. Stop smiling, Jack, I'm serious. This working girl wants to work and needs to support herself."

"Hey, Ivy, hasn't it been a good ride up 'til now?"

"Jack, you're not taking me seriously. I mean what I said."

"Is that some kind of subtle threat? What are you going to do? Walk away from me, Ivy? No one walks out on Jack Bauman and doesn't regret it later. Sure, you can walk, but you better think about your career prospects without me. The part you're in was a gift from me.

"We auditioned several women for the part you're playing and chose you. Gail Owens, one of your fellow cast members, was a leading contender but your audition aced her out at the last minute. I was looking forward to seeing *her* in the negligee."

"That probably explains Gail's coolness toward me on the set. I had no idea I displaced her in the competition for the part." Ivy paused a moment reflecting on Gail's obvious and understandable disappointment. "In any event, Jack, I think I've paid you back many times over."

"You think so? Let me tell you, there are lots of legs ready to spread for me and they all look the same when they part. You're nothing special, Ivy. Some nights you were a very average lay, but I didn't complain."

"Jack, let's not go this route. I've said what I had to. It's probably best that I leave now."

Ivy could see this conversation going into territory she didn't want to discuss.

"Maybe you should, Ivy. Just remember when that door closes it isn't the only one that shuts."

"Enough with your threats, Jack."

As Ivy rose to leave, Jack firmly grabbed her wrist. He pulled her toward him and pressed her close. She felt his hardness and his hands on her buttocks. He pulled her to the sofa and pushed her down on it.

"So, this is how you want to say goodbye, Jack?"

"Yeah, you know the drill."

"Let's do it right then. On your bed. Let's go."

Her inner rage was taking over. Bauman's lack of concern for her, outside the sexual realm, brought back memories of her brother's desertion. In her mind, the two men had taken cruel advantage of her.

She led him into the bedroom, pushed him down on the bed and pulled off his shoes, socks, and pants. She slipped out of her dress. Before mounting him, she took two ties from the drapes.

"I'm gonna tie your hands to the bed frame, Jack. We did this once before and you said it was the best fuck you'd had in months."

She tied his wrists to the headboard and mounted him. He pushed his hips up, making an effort at deeper penetration.

As he did this, Ivy stuffed a large cloth dinner napkin in his gaping mouth and squeezed his nostrils shut. He struggled for a few minutes but as his lips turned blue his struggle faded and eventually ended. He lay there with his eyes open but not seeing. His brain was gone. Anoxic damage.

She removed the napkin from his mouth, untied his wrists, and put his clothes back on. She next cleaned off the food cart that had been used to bring their dinner into the suite and wheeled it alongside the bed. She rolled his body onto the cart and pushed it back to the dining area. Ivy next tilted the cart and let the body fall near Jack's seat at the table. She dressed herself and then tidied up the bed area where the struggle had ended. She replaced the ties on the drapes.

Ivy cut a piece of steak from her unfinished portion and chewed it slightly. Next, she opened his mouth, pulled his tongue forward, and pushed the piece of steak down his throat. The CPR course she'd taken had emphasized pulling the tongue forward to favor access to the airway rather than the esophagus. She then used the handle end of her knife to push the piece of meat even further down. To confirm its position in his airway, and not his esophagus, she next squeezed his nostrils closed and blew a strong breath into his mouth, being careful to assure a tight seal where their mouths were joined. She observed no chest expansion, but did see some abdominal expansion. This confirmed that the piece of meat was obstructing his airway.

She called 911 and sat down on the sofa.

The police surveyed the scene and saw no reason to doubt Ivy's story. A beautiful actress having dinner in a movie mogul's suite tries to rescue the man with a Heimlich maneuver as he starts to choke on a piece of poorly chewed meat. Ivy's experience in a CPR class on resuscitation for bystanders included recognizing the need for a Heimlich maneuver, which in this case proved unsuccessful. She said she also tried mouth-to-mouth resuscitation and chest compression, but that too was unsuccessful.

The forensic police retrieved the piece of meat from Bauman's airway and bagged it for evidence.

Hotel management consoled a very shaken actress and saw to it that she was transported home once she was considered

reasonably recovered from the episode and discreetly questioned by the police.

Back at her apartment, Ivy took stock of the evening. The
greedy producer was no longer holding her career hostage.
Trouble was, the greedy producer was no longer in a position
to *further* her career. Getting the current film under her belt
would put her a bit farther ahead than where she was when
she showed up for that first audition. When the finished film
previewed and was seen by the critics, she'd find out if Ivy
Brandt had any currency in the film world. Kate McCallister
would then have to earn her bread and seek out work for her.

CHAPTER 43

Lester Brandt knew what the meeting was going to be about. Arnold Lasker was pissed off that he was going to have to deal with an unpleasant reality that he had no hand in creating. His purchasing department was going to have to bear the brunt of the mess along with his legal department. The only question was how much of the shit was going to fall on him.

Lester entered the office with a somber look on his face.

"Have a seat, Les."

The president got up from his desk, walked around it, and took a seat opposite Lester. His icy composure was off-putting.

"I had an angry surgeon in here a few days ago, Lester. It was the first I heard about a problem with a hip device. You should have clued me in as soon as you had an inkling something bad was coming our way. The surgeon caught me flat-footed. I don't like to be naked like that. It's embarrassing."

"You're right, Arnie. I let you down."

"Don't give me that schoolboy apology, Les. Your hang-dog expression doesn't mean anything in this office. Just tell me the story in all its gruesome detail."

Lester could see there was not going to be any easy escape route here.

"We've been using the Arnett hip prosthesis for over ten years. We use it exclusively. Recently, several patients have experienced premature device failure. The device is supposed to last a minimum of ten years and these failures were occurring after three or four years. That's all I can tell you. There are hundreds, maybe even a thousand, of these more recent devices out there, so I anticipate more failures."

Lasker's expression was unrevealing. As a seasoned executive he knew there were plenty of scapegoats between him and a problem like this. He was looking at one.

"I suppose AllCare is our supplier. Eric Dillon and company."

"That's right, Arnie."

"Have you discussed this with him? Do you have an explanation for the failures? Does Dillon have an explanation?"

"The device was given full FDA approval just last year after ten problem-free years. Now, several failures have occurred. They all were devices inserted in the last four years."

"Okay, what does that suggest, Les?"

Lester felt like a schoolboy being questioned in the principal's office. "The newer devices must be different."

"Okay. And who is supposed to be aware of any changes in the device? You? Dillon?"

"Dillon brings the devices into this country. We assume any change in the product would be brought to our attention by AllCare. We have no contact with the manufacturer. In this case that's in Vietnam. AllCare is a middleman. We're their customer. AllCare is a customer of the producer in Vietnam."

"That's helpful, Les. One last question, a bit off topic. I'm not naive. I used to do purchasing in my earlier life. Are you being paid by Dillon to buy the products he wants to push? Do you then encourage our surgeons to use that very same product? Do you offer them inducements? Think carefully, Les. If you are, it won't look good when the press starts to sniff around. In the record industry they used to call it 'payola.'"

"This is very difficult for me, Arnie. But, yes. You're right about that. Dillon has been sharing some profit with me. I don't have a defense. It was pure greed on both our parts. I socked away most of it, but Ivy found out about my cache and made off with half of it in our recent divorce settlement. She doesn't know the source of the money."

"At least you've leveled with me, Lester. I'll speak with our attorney and find out what our options are. I want the lawyer to tell me how much of the blame lies with AllCare. But now, and I mean right now, those payments to you from Dillon must end. We can't clean up the past but going forward your hands will be clean. Am I making myself clear?"

Lester looked like he'd aged a decade or two.

"Absolutely. I'll take care of that this afternoon. I appreciate your understanding, Arnie. It was foolish on my part. I never spent a dime of the money."

"Looking ahead, Lester, keep me posted on any developments."

CHAPTER 44

Two terrific seats at the Philharmonic were courtesy of a grateful patient who was out of the country. Gene and Leslie both loved classical music.

"Seats are not too shabby, Gene. You couldn't ask for a better evening at the Philharmonic."

"I needed something like this to take my mind off the hip joints. I had an unpleasant meeting with Gene Lasker, the Metro president. I let out my feelings about the hip prosthesis in his office. I must have sounded like some rabid college protester from the sixties. I won't apologize, but I vented more than I should have."

"It's funny, Gene, how life takes unexpected turns. Sometimes venting is all you can do. Other times two great seats drop in your lap and have restorative value. Let's just enjoy the evening."

"Let's."

They grabbed some frozen yogurt and brownies on the way to his apartment. Leslie knew this was the end of their run. Her feelings for Gene had never evolved into a real romance. They were good friends but the friendship wasn't going to take off in another direction. Leslie had good instincts about her female-male relationships. Now she had to find a kind way to convey that to him.

Later that night, sitting on her bed, the late-night news came on and after a few headline stories about China, Trump, and a tornado in Arkansas, the death of prominent movie producer, Jack Bauman, was featured in a forty-five-second clip. The story quickly recounted his rise to the top of the movie industry. Details of his death followed. He died in a freak accident in his hotel suite, suffocating on a piece of food lodged in his airway. He was having dinner with an actress featured in one of his movies being shot on location in Manhattan.

Leslie waited for the name of the actress, but it was never given.

The next morning *the Times* carried an extensive obituary on Bauman's life and career. It also recounted the tragic way he died and named the actress who was with him at the time: Ivy Brandt.

Leslie frowned. Ivy again. Was this purely accidental? Considering her suspicion that Ivy was somehow implicated in the disappearance of Cheryl Winter, this death immediately raised a question in her mind. She called Chan.

"Chan, did you read the Bauman obit in *the Times*?"

"Of course, I did. You're gonna make a point. I can feel it coming."

"Did you notice who was with him in the hotel room?"

"Yeah. Ivy Brandt. I see where this is heading."

"That's right, Chan. The very same Ivy we discussed last week as a possible killer. Makes you wonder, doesn't it?"

"Not really. The story was pretty complete. Police seemed satisfied."

"Come on, Chan. How hard would it be to stage the food choking episode she claimed to witness?"

"You're really going down this road? How could she pull this off?"

"Sure, he'd have to be restrained. Not too difficult if you're having kinky sex. Think about it."

"Okay, it's possible. I get your point."

"All we need is an angle that makes her a suspect. He was a very powerful man in the industry. Could do a lot for an aspiring actress. He could extract what he wanted in return for furthering a career."

"Boy, Leslie, you can build a case from next to nothing. If crime ever slows down the police may call on you to manufacture some crimes and save our jobs."

"Very funny, Chan. Just humor me a little longer. So why kill the goose that lays the golden eggs? Good question. The answer to that may be the reason that goose got cooked. I'm gonna look into that."

Leslie next called Diana Gold.

"Hi, Diana. This is Leslie."

"Hi, Les. Guess you heard about Bauman. Seems Ivy had a front row seat for this performance.

"Yeah, I read all about it in the paper this morning. Quite a night for our actress friend. Have you spoken to her?"

"No. Thought I'd give her a day off before hearing what really happened in that hotel suite."

"This isn't a social call, Diana. I was looking for some information. You know this reporter's mind never stops working. I'd like to talk to her agent. Would you happen to know her name or have her phone number?"

"Sure. I'll text it to you as soon as we finish this call."

"Thanks, Diana. Let's have lunch sometime this week. I'm anxious for some 'women talk.' Let's aim for Thursday. I'll call Angio's on Second Avenue for around one thirty, after the crowd thins out. I'll text you if it's a go."

"Sounds good, Leslie. See you there. Ciao."

Kate McCallister was next. A secretary answered and, after hearing she was from *the Times*, put her through to the agent.

"Hello, Ms. McCallister. I'm Leslie Nugent, a *Times* reporter and friend of Ivy Brandt. Can we talk for a few minutes?"

"Sure, Ms. Nugent. How can I help you? I suspect you're following up on the Bauman story in your paper this morning."

"That's right, Ms. McCallister. Can I call you Kate? Please call me Leslie."

"Kate's fine with me, Leslie."

"By the way, the story in *the Times* this morning isn't mine. This is more a personal matter with me. I'm looking for some information about Ivy's connection with Jack Bauman. For instance, was he responsible for her getting the part in the movie she's shooting?"

"You know Jack had a lot of connections and influence. He played a part in lifting Ivy out of her off-off Broadway play and into a serious movie. This was her big break. He had a hand in that."

"I understand, Kate. I'm also not naive; I'm sure it didn't come without a price. Was Ivy seeing Jack Bauman during this movie shoot?"

"You're touching on a sensitive subject, Leslie. I'm not going to tell stories out of school. Ivy is my client and a friend. Let's keep our distance from that aspect of her career."

"I understand. How about Ivy's future now that Jack is gone? Is she set up for a new role after the current shoot ends?"

"There's nothing on her schedule once this gig is over. I've been knocking on doors. Once the film comes out and she gets seen, that could give her a boost. Remember, she's a newcomer. It'll also help if she gets good reviews. This is a very competitive business, Leslie, and Ivy has plenty of well-known actresses in her age group looking for the same kind of parts she's seeking."

"Was she getting itchy wondering if Jack was going to

look after her? Did she express any concern that he hadn't found a role for her?"

"We talked a lot about the future, but her relationship with Jack was a very private matter. Ivy was very closemouthed about it. Jack Bauman had helped other young actresses get their careers off to a good start. That's all I can say on that score."

Leslie could feel the resistance Kate was putting up. She was not going to come out and say that Ivy's investment in Jack's pleasure was not yielding the dividend she expected. If Ivy had concluded that Jack was using her and didn't feel the need to offer her the prize she was after, she might very well have ended their relationship on an ugly note.

"That's all I have to say, Leslie. I wasn't a fly on the wall last night. I have no idea what transpired in that hotel suite. I talked to Ivy this morning, but she was too distraught to say very much."

"Thanks, Kate, you've been very kind. I respect your relationship with Ivy."

Leslie suspected that Ivy had not gotten what she expected from Bauman. As her film shoot began to wind down, she must have felt a need to have it out with Jack. All that time between the sheets and nothing to show for it.

CHAPTER 45

The out-of-town couple was in New York City to celebrate their anniversary. They did this every year; a two-night stay at the Holiday Inn in Midtown with a fancy dinner one night and theater tickets the next. The special occasion gave Lucy Grinnel an opportunity to wear some of the jewelry she'd accumulated over the years from her husband's deceased clients. She picked out a few pieces to wear to dinner tonight and put the remainder back in her jewelry case. She then slid the case under the mattress for safekeeping.

Police had Joseph Washburn under surveillance since several hotel guests had reported the theft of jewelry from their rooms over the past month. Washburn was a recent hire in the maintenance department and was assigned to the very floors where the thefts had occurred. His duties were to make minor repairs in the guest rooms, i.e., replace bulbs, repair shower curtain hooks, etc. He had access to all the rooms on the floors where he worked.

Tonight, he was in the Grinnels' room and easily found the jewel case under the mattress. He mused how guests hid things in places where any thief would look first. He unzipped the case and took the best-looking piece of jewelry. He then replaced the case. He usually only took a single piece so that theft was not immediately apparent to the guest.

He replaced a burned-out bulb in the bathroom and left. The surveillance camera in the hall saw nothing unusual. Washburn finished his work on the floor and then took the stairs down to the workers' locker room. As he was putting the evening's haul into his locker, two detectives appeared behind him and prevented him from closing the locker door.

"Mind if we look at what you just put in your locker, Joe."

One hour later, Washburn sat in a chair in an interrogation room in Manhattan's 43rd Precinct. Four pieces of jewelry were on the table. The hotel had been informed of the theft and faxed over a list of names of the guests staying on that floor. The hotel would inform each guest of the theft and recovery. A police officer would meet with the guests who claimed a loss. He'd ask them to first describe and then identify which piece of jewelry was theirs.

The process went ahead, and all pieces were claimed. The necklace claimed by Lucy Grinnel bore the initials CW and that caught the eye of Detective Ben Harrington.

With no particular reason to suspect another crime, Detective Harrington inquired about the disparity in initials between LG and CW. The Grinnels looked at each other and Clayton Grinnel answered the question.

"I'm a funeral director and sometimes I'm asked to bury or cremate a body for which there is no close family member. In those cases, I sometimes remove a trinket before disposing of the body. I see no reason not to."

"I understand, Mr. Grinnel. In this instance you had the body of CW and removed a necklace before what? Cremation? Burial?"

"I happen to recall this instance because the necklace was special. This was a body I cremated nearly a year ago."

"Mr. Grinnel, I'm not accusing you of anything. You can leave any time you wish. My interest lies in the identity of the person you cremated. We have a large number of missing person cases in the Metropolitan New York area and don't like to miss an opportunity to solve one."

"I understand. How can I help?"

"Tell me the circumstances of this cremation, as best you recall."

Grinnel was silent a moment and stared down at his shoes.

"I'm afraid it's a bit offbeat, Detective. By that I mean it's quite unusual. I never had one like it before or since. I got a call from someone. A man, I think. He wanted to *use* my cremation facility, no questions asked. I would have no direct involvement in his activity. He assured me he would have an expert in cremation accompany him. He offered to pay five thousand in cash. Sure, it was suspicious, but the money sounded good. I agreed. I guess that was foolish.

"The next evening two men arrived by car with a body in the trunk. They carried it inside and placed it on the crematorium table. I watched from across the room. All I know is that the body was wrapped in a heavy cloth. The head and neck were partially exposed. It was a woman. I don't recall anything else.

"A necklace hung down from the body's neck. This necklace. I removed it without anyone taking note. They were interested in the trappings of the room. I left before they carried out the procedure. An hour or so later one of the men handed me five thousand in fifty-dollar bills and the two left without saying a word."

"Okay. Now tell me about the men who delivered the body. Describe them."

"They were normal-sized guys. One had a beard and dark frame glasses. He wore a cap, but I could see his hair was dark. There wasn't anything unusual. The other guy I didn't see enough of to describe."

"How about the car?

"It was dark when they arrived. I can't say much about the

car. It was a four-door sedan. Nothing special. I'm sorry. I'm not being terribly helpful."

"Last thing. The woman's body. Anything special about the body?"

"Sorry, again. I only saw a partial head and neck. Probably a white woman. I didn't see her body so I can't offer any identifying marks. I don't think she was old. Oh, yeah. Her left hand hung out of the wrapping and had a cast, probably for a broken finger. Best I could tell."

"That'll do it, Mr. Grinnel. Call me if anything occurs to you that you didn't recall this evening. A word of warning: disposing of a body when you're unaware of the circumstances of the death could make you an accessory to a crime. *I think you know that.* I realize you were only letting someone use your facility. I don't expect there'll be any follow-up in this instance. Your cooperation is appreciated. Your action here was foolish but not criminally motivated. Here's my card. If you have a business card, I'd appreciate one. And thank you for your help."

Harrington knew that missing person cases were divided between the homicide and robbery divisions because they were so numerous and had no home of their own. He sent out an email to detectives in both those divisions alerting them that he had some information about a probable adult female MP with the initials CW. That was the best he could do. It was worth the effort.

Chan Young was reviewing his emails at home. His family was sound asleep. When Harrington's email appeared, he noted it but it didn't grab his attention. Then he remembered that Leslie had taken a recent MP case of his and set up a file for it on her desk. It was that woman from Metro. He recalled her name. Cheryl Winter.

It was almost midnight, but Leslie would want to hear about this case. He dialed her.

"I know it's late Leslie, but I have some news for you. A Detective Harrington from the 43rd has information about an adult white female MP with the initials CW. I texted him that we'd be in his office tomorrow morning at nine. I guess that's this morning."

"I can't wait to hear what he has to say, Chan. Now I'll never get to sleep. I have that folder on my desk here at home. Sometimes you get a break even when you're doing nothing."

CHAPTER 46

Leslie picked up a dozen assorted donuts and filled her thermos with the best French roast coffee. She and Chan were early for the nine o'clock but so was Ben Harrington. They retreated to a quiet interview room, got to work on the donuts and coffee, and listened as Harrington related the entire story of the amateurish jewel heist and the interview with Grinnel. He described the body much as Grinnel had, including the cast on her hand.

Leslie took particular note of the cast and Grinnel's guess that it was serving as support for an injured small finger. She thought back to Diana's anecdote about Ivy and her antagonist in college who'd had a finger injury before recanting a rumor about Ivy. Leslie wasn't sure what to make of it but didn't care for coincidences. Did this tie Ivy to the woman's murder? She recalled her conversation with Diana at Ivy's party.

Chan was the first to speak. Leslie knew it was best if the cops shared the news between them. She wasn't sure how Harrington felt about a lady reporter in the room with them.

"Incredible, Ben. You may have given us the key to help uncover a murder. I think we should ask Cheryl Winter's mother if she recognizes the necklace. We don't want to get too far out ahead of ourselves."

"Happy to help any way I can, Chan. The necklace has been logged in as evidence against the hotel jewel thief but I'm sure I can get it freed up for you."

"Ben, I sense your unease about Leslie sitting in with us. Trust me, she's a detective's best friend. We've worked together on several cases, and I dare say she's often out ahead of me on solving them. I trust her completely."

"Sorry if I let my old-fashioned cop's attitude about the press lump you in with your greedy colleagues, Ms. Nugent. Chan seems to have found a jewel in the crowd. Accept my apology."

"No apology needed, Detective. And accept my thanks for the jump start you gave the case we've been stalled on."

Chan and Leslie left with the necklace and headed to the apartment of Cheryl Winter's mother. That brief visit confirmed what they suspected: Cheryl was killed, cremated, and an unidentified man, doubtless disguised, was involved.

"Trouble is, Leslie, we're no closer to knowing who's involved in this murder. We're just filling in the picture at the periphery."

"I agree, Chan. It's frustrating but it convinces me we're on the right path.

CHAPTER 47

Love After Parting opened in New York, Los Angeles, and Chicago. The reviews were generally positive. It was a solid hit. The stars were given well-deserved praise, but the big surprise was the glowing review for Ivy Brandt. Even though her part was a supporting role, most reviews singled her out for special mention.

Ivy and Kate McCallister were having breakfast at a bagel shop the following day, reading reviews in the major papers.

"I knew you were good, Ivy, but not this good. You couldn't ask for a better way to jump-start your career. Congratulations, gal. I think we'll see some serious offers from the major studios as well as the independent film producers."

"I'm as excited as you are, Kate. I want to savor this moment before we think about the future."

The producers of the movie hosted a celebratory party at a popular Midtown Chinese restaurant. They took over the restaurant after it closed and had the kitchen and bar in full operation. The mood of the gathering couldn't have been more upbeat. The cast and crew were allowed to invite two guests each, so the place was jammed.

Ivy invited Diana and Leslie. Ivy was warmly congratulated by members of the cast and basked in the attention she was getting.

At the crowded bar Ivy rubbed shoulders with a tall, broad-shouldered, good-looking guy in a fine-checked cashmere sport coat and gray turtleneck. He turned to see who his elbow was butting.

"Pardon my elbow, miss. I'll get out of your way in a minute. I see my drink coming over."

Ivy flashed her winning smile and decided to check out the guy.

"Drinking alone, stranger? I'm surprised."

She saw a suntanned guy, clean-shaven, in his thirties, she guessed. She was surprised at how brazen she felt. That probably was a reflection of all the praise she'd been receiving. There was no wedding band so she figured he was fair game for the moment.

"I'm Ivy Brandt, a member of the cast. Did you see the movie?"

"Not yet. It didn't play where I was staying last week. I'm Doug Merchant, not a member of the cast or crew. I'm just a friend of Guy Wright, one of your producers."

Ivy was hoping he would keep up the conversation and take her away from the bar to some less crowded space.

"We've got the barman for a brief moment, Mrs. Brandt, so give him your order and we can retreat to some quieter place."

Ivy gave the barman her order for a margarita, straight up. While waiting for the drink she dug a little into his life story.

"What do you do, Mr. Merchant?"

"I'm in the entertainment field, much as you are. I'm a pitcher for the Mets. I'm the oldest guy on their player roster."

"Wow, I've never met a major league player. I haven't been much of a fan in recent years, but I *was* back in my high school days. Here comes my drink."

Ivy took her drink from the bar counter and waited for him to make a move steering them out of the densest part of the crowd. He did just that and they found a spot near a wall and a tall plastic plant, giving them relative privacy.

"Good move, Doug. I'm embarrassed not knowing a thing about the Mets. Let's just start simple. Am I crashing someone's party while talking to you like this?"

"Ivy, I'm a single guy, here on my own. *You're* not intruding. Am *I*?"

"Same story. I'm a single woman, recently divorced, unattached and trying to make it in the movies."

The conversation continued for nearly half an hour until one of the studio moguls got up on an elevated portion of the floor and made some effusive remarks about the cast and crew. When he got to Ivy, he was more lavish in praise. The crowd applauded heartily so she waved from the back of the room. He then moved on to praise others.

"Hey, I didn't realize who I was monopolizing. You probably want to dive into that crowd and enjoy the moment."

"Doug, I *am* enjoying the moment with *you*."

She reached into her purse and produced a small ballpoint pen. She penned her phone number on a napkin and handed it to him.

"I do have to mingle tonight but I hope you'll give me a call and get us together in a more cozy atmosphere."

"You can be sure I will, Ivy."

She walked to the crowd and disappeared into it. Doug just stood there a moment. He'd just met a beautiful, charming, friendly, unattached woman. She seemed genuinely interested in him and not self-absorbed, which encouraged him to dig deeper. Romance for a big-leaguer was not easy to sustain. He was on the road half the time during the season and when he *was* in town most of his evenings were committed to the game. Still, a woman like Ivy might be worth the effort.

Ivy caught up with Diana and Leslie in the crowd. Diana was quick to congratulate her and Leslie seconded the motion most enthusiastically.

Diana was sincere in her praise. "Ivy, you've really scored big with your first shot at a movie. There's no telling how far this'll carry you."

"That's a friend talking, Diana. Let's wait and see what the studios say in terms of offers. I'm happy with this opening burst but the follow-up will tell what it really means."

The three women were enjoying the high of the moment. Ivy's reserve, though understandable, couldn't dull the sense of celebration that rained down on her.

Leslie was curious about the guy Ivy had huddled with away from the partygoers. She teased her friend, "Who was that handsome guy we saw you making a play for? It looked like something was brewing, Ivy. Diana and I couldn't help wondering who you'd plucked out of the crowd."

"The guy's name is Doug Merchant. He's a baseball player."

Diana and Leslie repeated the name in unison. "Doug Merchant!" Diana continued on like a Beatle groupie, "He's probably the best pitcher in baseball and a shoo-in for Cooperstown."

Leslie weighed in with "Did you get his autograph?" She and Diana laughed out loud.

"Hey, I had no idea he was a celebrity. He's very modest. He never tooted his horn except to say he was the oldest player on the Mets' roster. I guess I missed my opportunity to drool on his shoes. I gave him my number and encouraged him to call and arrange to meet somewhere without a loud party atmosphere and my spying friends."

Leslie was supportive of Ivy's low-key approach. "I'm betting on a phone call in the very near future. Like, tonight or tomorrow. He seemed really interested in whatever you two were talking about."

Their threesome was interrupted by people Ivy knew from the production. As she turned her attention to her colleagues, Ivy looked back over her shoulder and asked Diana and Leslie, "What's Cooperstown?"

Later that night, back in her apartment, Ivy couldn't get Doug out of her mind. She hadn't felt like this in quite a while. It was a good feeling. She'd have to get some books about baseball and become a fan.

When Diana and Leslie left the restaurant, they strolled slowly in the general direction of Leslie's uptown apartment. It was a delightful autumn night, but they couldn't get Ivy out of their minds.

"You and I, Diana, are the only two women on this island who know what baggage that actress carries. My male friend, a homicide cop, knows what we know but I'd exclude him for the moment. Hard to reconcile tonight's Ivy with the one we've uncovered."

"You're so right, Leslie. I guess context is everything. For Ivy there are situations that bring out the Mr. Hyde in her. Otherwise, she's the genial, friendly Dr. Jekyll. I've read a bit about dissociative personality disorder and wonder if we're seeing one before our very eyes. Doug has seen Dr. Jekyll. We can only hope nothing triggers the other personality."

"I agree, Diana. I wanted to grab her and warn her about her alternative self. Maybe a real romance could exercise some control over that propensity. She was so damn charming tonight."

CHAPTER 48

Leslie had a good feeling about the prosthesis failure story. Her trip to Hanoi had given it some real bite. She felt it was time to take it to her editor, John Livingstone, to bring him up-to-date and get his advice on where to take it next.

She ran through what she had: the premature failures, the appearance of the prosthesis she examined with Gene, the tale out of Hanoi, and the roles of AllCare and Metro. She hesitated to bring Gene into the picture but realized that he would have a place in the story, not necessarily in any way complicit.

"The story is a keeper, Leslie. It has greed, patient tragedy, and oversight failure. Good ingredients for a front-page story. I'm not sure how it could have been prevented before someone got hurt. No one is going to benefit from this except the personal injury attorneys. Metro's and AllCare's liability carriers are going to look for ways to limit their payouts. The physician malpractice insurer will also be slithering around. The cast of players gets larger by the minute."

"My approach, John, has me trying to protect the surgeons by downplaying their role in the drama. I am friendly with the one who experienced the first failures. Am I being biased?"

"That's for you to decide. I ask my reporters to be professional at all times, you're no exception. Let me see the first draft. I think we can run with what you have. We seem to have the inside track here because of your doctor contact but that won't last forever. Get some more info and keep me posted."

"One last thing, John. I wonder if the hip joints are just the tip of the iceberg of the failed equipment at Metro. I thought I'd visit their repair shop and see if there were other pieces of equipment that had failed to live up to performance or durability expectations. Just a far reach but maybe worth a day in Metro's basement."

"Good thought, Leslie. Go to it but be careful. As the stakes grow larger the danger increases for the person shining the spotlight."

"I appreciate your encouragement, John, *and* the warning."

CHAPTER 49

After several disappointing calls to studio casting directors she knew quite well, Kate McCallister could sense she was not getting the friendly welcome she'd anticipated. Here she was, marketing what she believed was a hot property, and no one showed the slightest interest. Her next call was to Alvin Murray, an old friend who was casting properties for Netflix.

"Hi, Alvin. Kate McCallister. It's been a while since we spoke. How are you?"

"I'm doing great, Kate. Business is booming at Netflix. We can't find enough talent to fill the parts our writers create. We even welcome agents like you. Not like the old days when we told our secretaries to brush off agents."

"Well, Alvin, I'm representing Ivy Brandt. I'm sure you saw the rave review she got in *Love After Parting*. Ivy is—"

Alvin interrupted her. "Hold it right there, Kate. I read the reviews and I saw the film. She is a real talent. My concern is her drug problem. Is that under control?"

Kate was silent for a moment.

"What are you talking about, Alvin? There is no drug problem. Never has been. Where did you hear that?"

"It's out there on the street, Kate. You better smother it. It's gonna keep the big studios away from Ivy Brandt."

"Help me, Alvin. That's pure fabrication. I know Ivy Brandt. She's pure professional and would never jeopardize her career for a drug habit. She's never been involved in drugs of any kind. I've known her a long time. How can I get to the source of this ugly rumor?"

"I don't know, Kate. I'll take you at your word and give Ivy serious consideration for a big part here at Netflix. I mean it."

"Thanks, Alvin. I really appreciate your friendship. You know I wouldn't lead you down the garden path. Our relationship is too valuable to risk by lying about an up-and-coming actress's issues with addiction."

"I hope you get this straightened out, Kate. A rumor like this is a cruel way to smother a budding career."

Kate called Ivy and they met at Kate's office. After relating to her the dismal response she'd encountered at the major studios, Kate filled her in on her conversation with Alvin Murray.

"At least we know what we're up against, Ivy. Alvin will probably come up with a good part at Netflix so at least you won't be out of work."

Ivy maintained a calm demeanor but was seething with anger inside. The enemy wasn't the rumor; the enemy was the person who planted the rumor. She shared her suspicion with Kate.

"I can think of only one person who would benefit from my being shut out at the studios and might harbor pathologic jealousy over my success with *Love After Parting*. It has to be Gail Owens. She thought she had the part I was chosen for. Jack Bauman told me she was being seriously considered for the part but had to accept a lesser role after my audition."

"Could be, Ivy. Just don't do anything rash until I've had a chance to confirm that suspicion. Stay cool."

Ivy had no doubt that Owens was responsible. Who else had enough hate and jealousy to plant such a rumor? She was going to keep that knowledge to herself and plan a "proportionate response," as they say in the Pentagon.

"I'm glad your friend was willing to level with you, Kate."

Ivy had innocently snatched the part out of Gail's jaws after Gail came to believe, at least in her own mind, the part was hers. Containing her fury would not be easy for Ivy. She'd give Kate the few weeks she'd asked for.

CHAPTER 50

Leslie made an appointment to see Eric Dillon. Reluctant at first, Dillon saw more trouble from denying the reporter access than granting an interview. He was confident he could control the interview and limit any damage that might ensue.

AllCare's alternate executive offices were housed in a modern glass and steel six-story office building of their own in downtown White Plains, New York, just thirty miles from Manhattan. Leslie waited outside the president's office in a comfortable, soft, coffee-colored leather chair. She sipped the coffee offered to her by the attractive woman whose ID badge identified her as an administrative assistant. *The New York Times*, *Wall Street Journal* and *Business Week* lay on the coffee table in front of her chair. The atmosphere was businesslike but not without some human touches. Two large prints of paintings by Sargent hung on the wall facing her, flanking the door into the president's office. The door opened and a smiling Eric Dillon, in shirtsleeves, invited the reporter inside.

"Thank you for making the time to see me, Mr. Dillon. I'm sure you're a busy man."

Leslie cut right to the chase. "I've been with *the Times* a little over two years, Mr. Dillon. I'm a general news reporter, not a business reporter. I'm not here to collect a lot of statistical information."

Dillon settled down and sat back in his plush, high-back

desk chair. Leslie settled into one of the two chairs facing the desk. It was very comfortable.

"What *do* you want to talk about, Ms. Nugent? You mentioned something about prosthetic hips. That doesn't sound like a general news reporter's beat."

Leslie knew Dillon was being evasive. He was aware of the prosthesis problem but was going to make her take the lead getting there.

"We're both aware that there have been several premature Arnett hip joint failures this month at Metro. Since you supply Metro with the Arnett device, I'd like to know what you think the problem is."

"That's pretty direct and to the point, Ms. Nugent. I've heard some rumor about the failures but I'm not a tech person, so I can't offer an opinion I don't have."

"Okay, Mr. Dillon. It's my contention that you've squeezed the supplier in Vietnam so hard that he can only survive by reducing his expenses and potentially compromising the quality of the devices."

"That's an interesting thesis but even though you're not a business reporter I'm sure you know that getting a supplier to accept a reduced price is the way business operates. That's the capitalist system."

"Of course, you have to seek the lowest price for the products you buy. Problem is if you don't monitor the *quality* of that product as you drive the supplier to seek lower cost materials to make the product, it can lead to complications. Only when the device is badly compromised by substandard materials and inserted in hundreds of patients do you find out that you've passed the point of diminishing returns. Let me restate that: you reduce your cost, eventually receiving a compromised product which proves *more* costly owing to failures. Your return is diminished even though the product initially is more profitable."

Dillon was not one to cave in. He held his ground.

"For a nonbusiness reporter, you seem to have a good grasp of the concept of diminishing returns. It's been interesting talking to you, but I have little to offer in the way of information bearing on your hypothetical."

Leslie could see this conversation was going nowhere. She decided to give him a zinger and leave.

"Okay, Mr. Dillon. I understand your position. My trip to Hanoi was more illuminating than this trip to White Plains. I appreciate your time."

Leslie rose and abruptly left without a handshake.

Dillon's false smile had faded.

Walking to her rental car, she marveled at Dillon's duplicity. "Stonewall Dillon" she mused, never blinked until she mentioned Hanoi. Then she was out the door wondering what he made of her reference to a trip to Hanoi. She hadn't expected a *mea culpa* from him but, on the other hand, he never denied anything she implied.

CHAPTER 51

Sitting in her robe, reading *the Times* sports section over her now cold morning coffee, Ivy was still smoldering about Gail Owens when her phone rang. Call waiting raised her spirits.

"Hey, Doug. I was hoping you'd find that napkin in your jacket pocket and take this wild leap."

"I didn't need the napkin to prompt me, Ivy. I was thinking about calling ever since you left me standing alone and walked away to your adoring crowd."

"I actually looked in the paper today and saw that the Mets have a game tonight. You're listed as the starting pitcher and your record is eighteen and nine. How am I doing?"

"About as good as any fourth grader but you're getting into the game. I thought I'd sign on as your tutor and start at lunch today. I don't have to be at the ballpark until four thirty so that gives us a few hours to do lesson number one."

"How much tutoring do you think I'll need?"

"Can't tell until we do the first lesson. Just guessing, I suspect you'll need a lot. It depends on how you take to the material. Might even need some hands-on classes. We'll just have to see. How about Blake's Kitchen on Third Avenue and 26th at noon today. Gerry Blake is a fan. He knows me and always squeezes me in for lunch. You game?"

"Why not? I'll meet you outside the restaurant."

Ivy laughed at herself, flirting over the phone. She felt

like a college freshman enjoying the attention of a big man on campus.

The cab dropped her off a few minutes before noon. Doug was already waiting. She got out of the cab and walked toward him. Her slacks and sweater outfit showed her figure off to advantage. She wore a waist-length leather jacket. Her hair was loose, combed into pageboy style. Doug smiled his approval.

They greeted each other with a hug. His casual corduroys and quarter-zip sweater were in keeping with what she had anticipated.

"Two type As arrive before the appointed hour. Even our clothes are in sync. Is that a good or bad sign, Doug?"

"Guess we're a brother and sister pair, Ivy. Is that what you had in mind for us?"

"Not exactly. Depends how I take to baseball. Right now, I see people pouring into Blake's so I think we should hustle along inside. Get that baseball lingo? Hustle."

Gerry Blake greeted Doug like a brother and gave them a choice table in a far corner. Their conversation picked up where they left off at the party two days before. They both had a hard time taking their eyes off each other.

The baseball tutorial came with dessert. Ivy loved every minute of it. She was still amazed at her reaction to him. They'd just met Saturday night, and now, Monday afternoon, she was falling for the guy. She could tell he was more than just friendly. How did all this happen? Gail Owens was barely visible down the road. Doug Merchant had pushed her aside and almost eliminated any thought of her.

As they prepared to leave, Doug offered Ivy a seat at tonight's game in the owner's box. She was excited at the prospect but wondered if he could make it for two so she could bring a friend. A *girl* friend, she assured him.

"Done. You'll both sit in the owner's box. Don't eat dinner. There's lots of food there. Go to the special entrance for guests. I'll call ahead so they'll expect you. You'll love it."

"Great, Doug. I guess six thirty is a good time to get there. We won't hang around after the game so you don't have to rush and be concerned about us. Good luck, tonight."

Ivy called Diana but she was busy. She next called Leslie who was thrilled to go.

CHAPTER 52

Seeing a game from the owner's box was a new experience for the two women. They knew this was royal, first class. The stands down below them were a more real-world way to see a ball game. That didn't stop them from enjoying the luxury features that came with the box which was a large room with a big window facing the ball field. There were comfortable seats for watching the game and a long table with hot and cold buffet items. A small bar and well-stocked refrigerator completed the features of the box.

There were six other people in the room, including Roger Grossman, the Mets' principal owner, and his wife. Everyone was friendly and in high spirits before the game got underway. After introductions all around everyone knew that Ivy was the guest of Doug Merchant and Leslie was her friend.

Brad Grossman, son of the owner, assumed the role of Leslie's host. He was a forty-year-old attorney with a small firm in Manhattan that specialized in business law. Brad's accomplishments were proudly revealed by his father when he saw how friendly his son and Leslie were becoming. Leslie learned that Brad had been an NCAA second team All-American in soccer at Harvard and had received a Bronze Star from two tours with the marines in Afghanistan between college and law school. Brad was embarrassed by his father's boasting but had obviously been through this before.

Brad had never married.

Leslie was impressed by his modesty and easy manner.

His sandy hair was loosely combed. She found his brown eyes warm and inviting. He was an inch or so under six feet and seemingly well-built.

They were enjoying each other's company like old friends at a reunion. Leslie so far measured up quite well against any women in his experience. Ivy glanced over at the pair every once in a while, and smiled whenever Leslie caught her eye. Ivy was being absorbed into the owner's circle of friends who were interested to hear about her movie making experience.

Eventually the game got underway. Everyone's attention moved to the ball field. Doug was hooked up in a pitcher's duel with the Braves' starter. The game was scoreless through four innings.

Brad and Leslie used every moment, when action was suspended, to get better acquainted. Leslie, at first, felt like poor Cinderella being courted by the prince but over time this feeling evaporated. Her confidence restored, she comfortably handled her share of the conversation.

With the Mets leading 3-2, Doug came out of the game after seven innings. It would be up to the bullpen to save this victory for the Mets and Doug. The final two innings were very exciting as the Braves tied the game in the ninth but lost it when the Mets' catcher homered in the bottom of the inning to end the game. A Mets victory but no win for Doug since the tying run in the ninth took him out of contention for the decision.

The crowd in the box celebrated the victory along with the packed stadium. Brad explained to Ivy and Leslie why Doug wouldn't get the win in spite of his splendid performance. His quest for a twenty-win season would depend on his last three starts of the year.

As they all prepared to leave, Brad got Leslie's phone

number and said he'd be calling in a day or two. The evening had been a success on two scores for Leslie: a novel way to watch a game and meeting a very special guy.

Leslie and Ivy cabbed to Ivy's Midtown apartment. There was a lot to talk about on the way. Leslie again found Ivy charming and a good listener. She was ever trying to reconcile Ivy's past with her present person. They were becoming quite good friends, but she was troubled by her suspicion about the actress's violent acts. It was hard to dismiss what she knew.

Ivy couldn't wait to talk to Doug. She hoped he'd call tonight. The cab continued uptown to Leslie's apartment after letting Ivy out.

CHAPTER 53

Still no bites from the big studios. Kate McCallister had to chase down this rumored drug problem to its source. She called Desmond Walcott, the casting director who had recommended Ivy for the part in *Love After Parting*. They agreed to meet for drinks that evening at a convenient bar.

The bar they chose was slow on a weekday evening, so they had their pick of booths.

"You certainly chose a winner casting Ivy in *Love*. She was terrific. Why no call since that film hit the streets?"

"You know, Kate, if I had my way she'd have been signed for several pictures. My crew of casting helpers put the kibosh on it. They said there was a rumor of some drug problem, and they didn't think we should take a chance on her. I was stunned because she never seemed a bit high while we made the film. I just couldn't go against my staff. We passed over her even though she was the choice candidate for a big role."

"I'm trying to track down the *origin* of the rumor, Des. Is there anyone in your group who might have a handle on the source?"

"I think you should talk to Josh Mintz. He's a streetwise guy and was the one most adamant in our group against casting Ivy. I have his number on my phone."

Kate reached Mintz and he agreed to see her in private, after hours, in the casting team office. The office was closed by the time they met so they had all the privacy they wanted. Mintz was a nervous type with an eclectic array of tattoos on his thin arms. He didn't hesitate to tell Kate where he first heard the drug rumor.

"A group of us who hang out together were drinking beer after hours in this very office. One of the actresses who hangs with us brought up Ivy Brandt's name and told the group she was a closet drug user. She said Ivy used the powder on the set of *Love* and managed to conceal that from everyone on the set. On one occasion, though, Ivy was seen sniffing the powder in her dressing room, unaware of being seen by a cast member. The group was surprised but drug use is so prevalent among theater people that no one bothered to challenge the news."

"And the name of this actress?"

"Gail Owens. A fellow cast member of Ivy's." He paused a moment then had a question of his own. "Why are you chasing this down, Ms. McCallister? Are you questioning Gail's information?"

"Exactly! I know Ivy Brandt and there's no way she's a drug user. Gail Owens has a bone to pick with Ivy and has chosen a very vicious way to pursue it. The story won't end here, you can be sure. Thanks for your cooperation, Josh. Call me if I can be of any help to you."

She handed him her card and left.

Kate's call confirmed Ivy's suspicion. She began to conjure an antidote to Gail's poison.

CHAPTER 54

Metro Hospital sprawled over several city blocks. Its conglomerate of buildings dated from as far back as the late nineteenth century with some as recent as the past decade. There was no rhyme or reason to the architectural stylings.

Leslie approached the information desk at the main entrance to the hospital. When she asked the clerk behind the desk to direct her to the Building and Grounds Department, she was handed a detailed map of the hospital campus. The clerk circled in red an area labeled "B&G." Leslie began her trek.

Fifteen minutes later she arrived at a building with a sign over the door indicating that this was the B&G building. It was quite large and looked like a place where trucks and other kinds of heavy-duty machinery would feel at home. She found a portal identified as the building's entrance for people who had business inside. She went in and found no greeter or traffic cop to steer her to the repair shop. Leslie set about finding it on her own.

Eventually she encountered a friendly worker who offered help. Within minutes she found herself standing in front of a plexiglass window speaking to a woman through a porthole.

"I'm looking for the area where equipment repairs are done. I'd like to speak to the person in charge of the area."

The woman on the opposite side of the window looked her over and decided Leslie represented no threat to the equipment moving in and out. She dialed a number on her cell phone and shortly thereafter a large man in an oil-stained coverall came into the area through a nearby door labeled "Private." His nametag identified him as Cary Horton, shop steward. They exchanged introductions. Leslie explained the reason for her visit and saw no defensive reaction in Horton's eyes.

Leslie was invited to follow him into a very large, and noisy, machine shop.

"Is there some place we can sit and talk for a few minutes before you show me around?"

Horton pointed to a door labeled "Shop Steward" and ushered Leslie into his office. She welcomed the opportunity to sit down and relax for a few minutes. Horton welcomed the opportunity to get a better look at his guest.

"Cary, I'm Leslie. I'm a reporter doing a story about hospital equipment problems, if any. I thought this might be a good place to start. You're under no obligation to talk to me. I'm interested in anything you can tell me about recent problems. I'm sure a busy hospital is hard on its equipment. I'm curious to know if problems have become more prevalent in recent years."

"Interesting question. I've been here nearly fifteen years and I'd have to say that problems with some equipment have definitely increased. Let me give you an example. Respirators are in use all over the hospital; in the ICUs, CCU, recovery rooms, emergency room, general patient areas, operating rooms. We have a large number of respirators in this department awaiting repair today. I'd say that number far exceeds the number we had here just two or three years ago."

"What accounts for that, Cary?"

"That's simple. The respirators are not as durable as those we saw just a few years ago."

"Does that mean the hospital is buying inferior equipment? Why would they do that?"

"They're buying the same *brand* respirators they've been buying for years but the product is not the same. Trust me. We repair them and we know that certain parts are failing now that we never saw fail before. These newer versions must be less expensive so purchasing goes that route. *They* never see the failures. It's gotta be a bottom-line decision."

"Who's the supplier, Cary?"

"AllCare. Who else? They supply Metro with everything Metro uses. We don't buy the equipment; we just fix it when it fails. I wish the guys in purchasing talked to us occasionally. Maybe it'd make a difference; maybe it wouldn't."

"Cary, you've been really helpful. Now maybe you can show me around. I'd like to see that graveyard of respirators."

The tour put Cary's comments in context. Metro had a lot of respirators awaiting repair or burial. They looked relatively new but obviously were suffering from premature disease. Cary guided Leslie back to the hospital main entrance.

The trip to B&G had provided a meaningful companion piece to the hip device story. The focus was shifting over to AllCare.

CHAPTER 55

A Saturday night house party in Hoboken would have been an ideal first date with Brad Grossman but he was legitimately unavailable. Leslie asked Diana to be her date and the workaholic attorney accepted.

The host was a friend of Leslie's in a large apartment in a recently renovated tenement in downtown Hoboken, courtesy of her real estate broker father. She and Leslie had been friends ever since the fifth grade.

The local fire marshal wouldn't have been pleased to see a crowd of this size in the cozy apartment. Leslie and Diana were soon parted by the swarm of thirty- and forty-somethings moving like a tide from one drink station to another with a brief stop in between at one of the sushi tables.

Leslie angled to the nearest beer cooler, bared one arm, and had to reach deep into the ice water several times to find a beer she recognized.

"Good dive, lady. I was just going to reach in and grab one for myself. Were there any others submerged in there?"

Leslie found herself face to face with a rugged looking six-footer in a black boatneck sweater.

"Let me dive back under and see if I can grab one for you."

Leslie again put her arm into the freezing water and after a few seconds came up with a mate for the beer she'd pulled out for herself.

"Incredible, miss. A death-defying rescue in this frozen body of water."

Drying her arm off on a convenient towel, Leslie introduced herself. "I'm Leslie Nugent, audacious diver into freezing waters."

"And I'm Clay Webster, grateful recipient of this rrrrreally cold brew."

After establishing that they were each flying solo, they maneuvered to a wall location where they could talk without fear of being swept away in the human tide. Leslie identified herself as a news reporter and Clay indicated that he was the owner of a wholesale food company.

Clay gave her a brief rundown on how he got into the business and how little he knew about it until he actually had skin in the game.

Leslie kept him talking. "What's the aspect of the business that came as a surprise?"

"I'm not naive, Leslie. I'm relatively new at the game so I realize I have to start at a low rung and begin my climb. I'm quite willing to do that. I've built a good clientele at nursing homes, rehab facilities, hospices, and assisted living facilities. But the top rung is the large hospital. That's where I've hit a wall. Metro Hospitals is what I want to service, and I can't even get my foot in the door." He paused and looked at her inquiringly. "Are you sure you want to hear this?"

"Clay, I'm all ears. I think you're just getting to the good part from my reporter's perspective."

"Okay. One company services the Metro system. That's an enormous business. Millions of dollars in food supplies for the system. The company is AllCare. That's a medical supply company but it also supplies Metro with its food. There is no competition because Metro doesn't let any competitors in the door."

"How does this happen, Clay? And why? Wouldn't other

companies provide some price competition? Maybe even some better products?"

"Ah. Now you're at the critical point in the story. In this business, if you want a situation like AllCare's, you have to pay for it. The traffic cop is the Metro purchasing agent. He decides who services the hospitals. Buy him, own him, and he makes you his preferred supplier. He grants you monopoly status or at least a near monopoly. Clay Webster can only look in from the other side of the moat."

Clay stopped and gave Leslie a look that said, "now you know how this game is played."

"Clay, you don't know for a fact that the purchasing VP has been bought. Do you? You're just voicing your suspicion. Right?"

"You're right, but that's the best explanation I can come up with for the relationship between Metro and AllCare."

Leslie decided she'd had enough dark education for one evening. She didn't want to ruin Clay's evening any more than she had by letting him vent on this vexing subject.

"I think I better find the girlfriend I came here with, Clay. I'm sure she's wondering what happened to me. Clay, I'm glad we met. I learned a lot and really appreciate the insight you shared with me. I hope you find a way to break into that sealed off hospital market."

"Sounds like you're moving on, Leslie. I was hoping we'd have more time together."

"Bad timing, Clay. I've just started seeing a guy and I want to play that out before I get involved with another guy."

Leslie turned and dissolved into the crowd.

CHAPTER 56

The ball landed on the green but rolled beyond the hole into some tough grass. The seventh hole at Fallsview Country Club was a very difficult par three.

"Nearly had it, Luke. I guess the eight iron would have been a better choice. Would have been better to play it short and not worry about the trap."

Luke Rollins was Eric Dillon's guest. He'd been sent by the Ross-Wagner attorney to meet with Eric. Dillon's concern had sounded serious enough to merit high-level attention at the giant shipping company. Rollins was one of the company's top fixers and a decent golfer.

Five feet seven and slightly overweight, Rollins hardly looked like a guy with a twelve handicap. His fast-receding hairline was concealed under the brim of his cap which helped him pass for under fifty even though he'd seen that birthday a decade ago. He was pleasant looking with blue eyes. Men and women found him appealing for his easy smile and gift of gab.

"No one behind us, Eric, so why don't we take a break? You can elaborate on the concerns that brought me out here."

"Okay, Luke. Everything was going along just fine at Metro. You know the background of AllCare's relationship with Metro and our arrangement with Lester Brandt, so I'll spare you a long preamble. Lester had a girlfriend for several years. I guess she knew he and Ivy, his wife, were heading toward divorce. She realized that marriage to Lester was not in the cards and wanted a generous payout as she went out the door.

"She apparently had a strong suspicion, without proof, that Lester was squirreling away some serious money in the Caribbean. She threatened to tell Ivy about it in exchange for having the wife share that cache with her when it became part of the divorce settlement. Ivy's divorce attorney would find the money. This could bring AllCare's under-the-table payment scheme to Lester out into the open and expose us to serious legal charges. My mother-in-law's role here could be embarrassing."

"How much did this woman know about the money, Eric?"

"Just enough to set an attorney after it. I called the home office. The woman was taken care of. You may have been involved, Luke. I don't know. Unfortunately, information about the money still somehow got to Ivy's lawyer and it became part of the divorce settlement. Fortunately, Ivy doesn't know the *source* of the money."

"Okay, what's next?"

"A competitor in the food supply business has been frustrated by Lester whenever he tries to get his foot in the door and grab a small piece of the Metro business. He threatened Lester about challenging AllCare's monopoly position and hinted about going to the attorney general to voice his suspicion about a bribe being paid by AllCare. He doesn't have any hard information about a bribe, but the situation makes that scenario plausible."

"So, that's another soft threat. Keep going."

"You know about the hip joint problem. That's bad enough by itself, but the orthopedic doctor who has seen several of the unfortunate patients is making a stink about Metro and collusion with AllCare in pushing the defective device on the orthopedists. He's a bit shaky and has a history of instability. I worry that he brings too much light to shine on Lester Brandt."

"Okay, another potential concern. Are we done? I'm ready to hit my ball out of that mean rough."

"One last item. A newspaper reporter has gotten wind of the hip joint issue. She knows the orthopedist who identified the first few cases. She's pursuing the story and has even visited the factory in Vietnam where the devices are manufactured. She's chasing down the question of why the devices are failing. That focuses her right on the AllCare relationship with Metro and Lester Brandt. I recently heard she visited Metro's repair shop and found a large number of defective respirators. I suspect she's gonna build a case about poor purchasing oversight and, in the process, expose more about AllCare and Metro than we can afford.

"I say 'we' because a scandal like this will hurt my wife, Alyssa's daughter; maybe not legally, but certainly socially."

Luke headed to the cart and picked out a club from his bag. He turned to Eric and gave no hint of great concern over the matters Eric had laid out.

"I recorded our conversation, so don't worry about my recall. I'll bring the whole mess to our top executives and come up with a plan. I understand your concern, even if the threats are still only just beginning to surface. Now, I'm gonna chip out of the grass and hope I don't roll too far downhill."

His chip shot rolled only two feet beyond the hole and his putt for par was dead center.

CHAPTER 57

Luke Rollins, Marjorie Bannister, and Alyssa Ross sat at a conference table in Ross's office. The two women listened intently as Rollins reviewed the concerns Eric Dillon had presented to him the day before. Ross, owner and president of Ross-Wagner, and Bannister, her executive VP and personal attorney, had agreed to meet with Rollins on short notice. AllCare was a very valuable property, a legitimate business that allowed her daughter and son-in-law to live comfortably with no obvious connection to the Ross-Wagner company.

Dillon knew the score. He was the nominal owner of All-Care but his mother-in-law subtly exercised considerable control while staying in the shadows. AllCare was hugely profitable, largely owing to the monopoly position at Metro she'd "purchased" using Eric as the front man. A large legitimate business was also valuable as a place to start the process of laundering money generated by illicit activities. A steady flow of money harvested from Ross's drug traffic was mixed with the largely cash business generated by food sales to employees and visitors, as well as other retail businesses in the hospitals.

Bannister was first to respond. "The Arnett horse is out of the barn and the patient damage incurred will be dealt with in traditional ways. It's going to be a mess, but we have to accept it. Dillon apparently let his ego bring about this problem. He squeezed his source harder than he needed to and now will have to pay the price for his greed. For the moment he'll just have to absorb the punches for AllCare."

Ross agreed with Bannister's assessment and wanted to move on.

"The mistress has been taken care of, unfortunately too late for Lester Brandt. As long as his wife doesn't know about the source of the money she's shared in, she's not a problem. Am I right on this Marge?"

"Yes, Alyssa. Her ignorance is a shield against any claim for taxes by the IRS. She received a portion of the money as a domestic support obligation, otherwise she'd be an accomplice in a tax evasion scheme. Her attorney will keep her from snooping around, trying to understand where her ex had gotten the money. She's in the clear."

Alyssa offered an approach to the unhappy potential competitor. "The business rival is a more direct threat. He's aiming right at the under-the-table payments and could cause trouble even though he has no hard evidence. I suggest we talk to him and offer a small piece of the Metro food business in exchange for him going away quietly."

"Good approach, Alyssa. No need to use a stick when a carrot will do the job." Marjorie smiled.

Rollins offered an approach to the fuming physician. "I think the guilt-stricken orthopod will see it's to his advantage to maintain a low profile. I'll speak to him and convince him AllCare and Metro will be chastened by this mess and so his ranting from the sidelines is unnecessary and can only shine more light on his role in the episode."

Bannister focused their attention on the reporter and presented her as the most dangerous threat.

"The woman reporter bothers me. I know their style. They're tenacious and will turn over every rock they find. The payments to Lester Brandt are just what the reporter would like to sink her teeth into. We have to keep her from digging too deeply into this failed hip joint story. What do you think, Alyssa?"

"I agree with you, Marjorie. But first, Luke, what's the reporter's name?"

"I have it written down here." Rollins looked through some notes he carried in a folder. "Here it is. Leslie Nugent. She's with *the Times*."

Alyssa smiled and shook her head from side to side.

"Okay. I know this woman. I had an experience with her when she was doing a story on our drug manufacturer in Yonkers several years ago. I had to warn her off. She wound up the story to her satisfaction, before she got too close to our involvement in the operation. If she hadn't, a more direct approach might have been necessary to keep her from following the trail back to this organization."

It was Marjorie's turn to offer a solution. "We need to know how close she is to unraveling the AllCare scheme. That'll be your job, Luke. A tail and a listening device in her apartment might be helpful."

Alyssa felt the meeting had been productive. She summed it up neatly. "I can accept a newspaper story that unmasks AllCare's role in the hip joint mess as long as it stops before it exposes the payola to Lester Brandt. The hip joint mess will be the price to pay for Dillon's greed, but it needs to stop there. That's all for today."

"Before we break, Alyssa, I have one concern we didn't cover." Luke Rollins drew everyone's attention.

"Lester Brandt is a weak link in the chain. He obviously knows everything about the payments and could blow the whistle on Eric Dillon if pressed by some investigator or attorney. Dillon thinks he's shaky. The money under the table is a problem. I think Brandt has to go. Without him, an investigation would never get to Dillon. No payee; no payor. As I mentioned, Brandt's divorced wife knows he had hidden money but has no knowledge where it came from."

Alyssa was weighing the proposal.

"If Brandt is removed AllCare loses its valuable insider at Metro. Will we be able to co-opt his successor?"

"We did it once, why not a second time?" Rollins responded.

Alyssa wanted to wind up this discussion.

"Is he worth a hit? What does the group think?"

Both heads nodded in assent.

CHAPTER 58

She didn't recognize the caller's name on her landline phone but decided to take the call anyway.

"This is Leslie. I hope you're not going to ask for a donation."

"A donation would be fine, but that's not why I'm calling. You obviously don't recognize my name. I'm the guy you pulled from the freezing water last week in Hoboken. Well, pulled my beer from the icy water. Does that ring a bell?"

"Oh, yeah. The food supply guy. Now I remember. You gave me a brief rundown on how the seamy hospital business works. Actually, I appreciated it and felt bad about running off as you were just beginning to hit on me."

"No hard feelings Ms. Nugent. I tracked you down through our hostess that night. I'm Clay Webster."

"And I'm Leslie, Clay. What's on your mind?"

"I sensed you were interested in the matter I expounded on, so I thought you'd be interested in some follow-up."

"I really was and *am* interested, Clay. Let's hear it."

"A gentleman came to my office and had a proposal for me. If I would agree to cool my jets about being locked out of Metro, he would arrange for me to receive a contract to supply Metro with a sizable portion of their food supply needs. He mentioned the figure, twenty to twenty-five percent. All I had to do was let my concern about payoffs die and shake his hand. I took his hand."

"So, someone with clout was buying your silence. Sounds

like your understanding of how the game is played was given credence. Someone high up is trying to peacefully gain your acquiescence to the purchasing arrangement existent at Metro. I inserted *peaceful* in there because sometimes deals like this come at the expense of physical discomfort. Depends on whom you're dealing with."

'Leslie, you said it better than I ever could have. My conclusion was the same as yours. Just thought you'd like to hear this follow-up to our brief conversation last week. By the way, that guy you started seeing didn't turn out to be married with three kids in New Jersey, did he?"

"Sorry, Clay. If something like that does materialize, I hope you'll be sure to take my call. And thanks for the follow-up. I appreciate it."

CHAPTER 59

Gail Owens's address in Brooklyn wasn't difficult to find, nor was the doorman at her building paying close attention to the few people coming and going through the lobby at this late hour. Ivy checked the mailboxes and found Gail's apartment number. She rang the doorbell and stepped aside, out of view of the peephole in the door.

When Gail asked who was there, she replied, "A friend of Josh Mintz." That satisfied Gail.

When she started to open the door, Ivy threw her weight against it. The door slammed into Gail with sufficient force to knock the stunned woman to the floor. Ivy shut the door behind her and was on top of Gail before she even started to get up. Ivy quickly turned her on her stomach and tied her wrists together behind her with a preformed loop of rope. It all happened so fast that Gail hardly put up any resistance. Ivy smiled as if she'd won a calf roping contest at a rodeo.

"Before you ask, let me introduce myself, Gail. I'm Ivy Brandt, your acting colleague. The one you put out a rumor about a drug habit on. That was a bad decision."

A terrified Gail managed a breathless question, "What do you want from me? An apology?"

"Oh, a lot more than that, Gail. I'm gonna let you up now and then I'll tell you what you're going to do for me."

Ivy got off Gail's back and stood up. She let Gail struggle to her feet with her hands still tied behind her back. Once the captive was upright, Ivy placed her in a chair and pulled one over to sit facing her.

"A few ground rules before we start. I'll gag you if you scream. Any effort to escape will be dealt with in a most harsh manner. I know about the rumor you started but I'm not sure why you felt so inclined."

Gail overcame the shock of Ivy's attack and snarled at her.

"You *stole* that part in *Love After Parting* from *me*. It was mine and you only got it by fucking Jack Bauman."

Ivy was cool and composed.

"I don't need to explain anything to you, but I will. I was invited to audition, and the casting director thought I was perfect for the part. I didn't know *anything* about anyone else they were considering. I assumed they were looking at other actresses, but the casting director wanted *me*. I only fucked Jack Bauman *after* a contract was in my hands. That's all I have to say about that. You can take it or leave it.

"Now, here's what you're going to do for me. You're going to write identical letters to casting agents at each of five major movie studios telling them that you, Gail Owens, were responsible for a rumor accusing Ivy Brandt of being a drug user. Your motivation was jealousy over her being awarded a role you wanted in *Love After Parting*. You'll apologize for misleading people in the industry. I have the text of the letter here for you to copy and sign. I'm going to sit here until you finish the letters. I have five stamped and addressed envelopes which I'll mail after I leave. Here's a pen and paper. I'm going to untie your hands after I tie your ankles and place a noose around your neck to discourage any attempt to evade my directions."

Ivy placed the noose and sat in a chair behind Gail with the rope in her hands. She tightened the noose to convince

Gail that resistance was ill-advised, then untied her hands and told her to begin writing the brief letters.

Once the letters were signed and placed in the envelopes Ivy removed the noose but left the ankles tied to give her a head start before Gail could make any effort to stop her. She pocketed the original letter to show to Kate McCallister.

"I'm taking your cell phone, Gail. I'll FedEx it back to you along with this disconnected landline handset. I hope this is the last time we'll meet."

Once out on the street Ivy quickly walked several blocks before dropping the letters in a mailbox and hailing a cab.

CHAPTER 60

It was early evening and the newsroom staff were beginning to thin out. Sitting at her desk in the open newsroom, Leslie stared at the blank screen on her computer. A major story was taking form for her. It had started with insider knowledge about the hip joint problem but had expanded to include All-Care's greed as the root cause of the device failure. Now the likelihood of payola as the way AllCare secured a monopoly position at Metro was adding a dimension to the story. She had no proof of payola so that part would be kept out of the story until she found convincing evidence.

What am I missing here, she mused. *AllCare and Eric Dillon are the villains, but what about the guy buying Webster's silence? Was he an emissary from Dillon? Or are there other players in the game?*

Leslie tried to imagine other scenarios but was coming up short. She needed to know more about the company's history. She woke up her computer and put AllCare in the Google search bar. She was about to hit the enter button when her phone rang. Ivy Brandt's name showed on the screen.

"Hey, Ivy. I'm glad you called. What's up?"

"Leslie, I'm free for dinner and wonder if you can be dragged away from your desk to share some Szechuan take-out in my place. I have white wine in the fridge and fresh fruit for dessert. There's nothing for you to bring but yourself. Now, walk away from that computer and head over here."

Leslie hesitated. Instead of quickly agreeing as a good

friend would, something gave her pause. She decided to decline the invitation and offer some pressing work issue as an excuse.

"Wish I could, Ivy, but I'm facing a looming deadline on a story that's beginning to boil over."

"Okay, Les, I'm giving you a rain check. No sweat. Would've been a relaxing evening, but there'll be other opportunities."

"I wish I could break free, but tonight just doesn't work for me."

The conversation ended and Leslie reflected on her hesitancy. She and Ivy had become good friends but there remained a nagging unease about Ivy's potential to change from the charming, warm, bright woman into a person she didn't know, with a propensity for violence. To say she was afraid to be alone with Ivy in her apartment was a stretch but something akin to caution was certainly operative here.

CHAPTER 61

Brad Grossman could only guess what Leslie's food taste was. Playing it safe, he chose a popular restaurant with an eclectic menu. The decor was tasteful American all the way with lush carpeting and excellent soundproofing. They'd have no trouble hearing each other and that was the primary purpose of this first real date.

Leslie was determined not to let the date turn into a business dinner with her using his legal experience to answer the many questions she had about AllCare. Tempting, but the wrong tack to take with a guy she wanted to get to know better.

The meal was excellent. In conversation they each wanted to let the other know that the person opposite was willing to reveal quite a bit of personal information, a sign of trust and interest.

When Brad asked about her current projects the conversation veered into the territory she'd been trying to avoid: AllCare. Brad could understand her need to better appreciate the company's background history. He gave her a few sources to use and offered to do a quick search of his own. He admitted this was basic ABC for him, so it was no inconvenience. Leslie gently turned down his offer and steered the conversation back onto the personal tack they'd been cruising on.

The evening was a total success. She and Brad agreed to spend a day in the Metropolitan Museum of Art the following weekend. The cab ride back to her apartment included some frisky play in the back seat, a prelude to more serious action on a subsequent date. No need to rush ahead.

CHAPTER 62

Working away on a large bowl of cherries while watching a mystery on PBS in her darkened living room, Kate McCallister paused the recording. She marveled at how her message box had suddenly become a hot spot in her universe. Several major studios had discovered drug-free Ivy and wanted to see if she'd be interested in considering several roles they had in mind for her.

Kate was stunned by the sudden surge of interest in her previously dormant property. She hadn't heard from Ivy in over a week but now would take the initiative and find out what was new in the actress's world. She pushed the cherries aside, reached for her phone on the table in front of her, and brought up her contact list. Ivy answered on the second ring.

"Hi, Kate. It's Mets four, Cubs two, in the sixth inning. Doug just came out after a strong performance. This could be win number twenty at long last. What else did you want to know?"

"Ivy, you've become a late in life Met groupie. Are you wearing your Mets cap while you watch the game on TV?"

"Of course. I'm loyal through and through. I've been meaning to call you, but I was hoping you'd have a reason to call me first. Looks like you do."

"Tell me why the large studios in Hollywood, all of a sudden, are hot for your body. What are you not telling me?"

"I'm gonna send a photo of a letter to your phone. That'll

explain everything." After a brief pause Ivy continued, "I just sent the photo to you. Read it and call me back. Okay?"

"The suspense is killing me."

Kate read and reread the emailed photo/letter. The fog cleared and she understood why her inbox had gotten busy. She called Ivy.

"So, Gail realized that confession is good for the soul. I'm sure there's more to the story, Ivy, so let me hear it."

"You remember *The Godfather*? I made her an offer she couldn't refuse. Simple as all that. Let's skip the details. Okay?"

"Okay. No details needed. The letter worked. I'll be busy sorting out offers but it looks like you're gonna be a busy lady the next few years. I'm glad you were able to work your way out of the hole Gail dug for you. Someday you'll fill me in on the details. Now, I'm heading back to *Masterpiece Mystery*. Enjoy the great news."

The Mets won, 6-2, and Doug had his twentieth win. Ivy called to congratulate him.

CHAPTER 63

Rain was falling forcefully. Without an umbrella, Lester Brandt eagerly got into the first cab that drove up to the curb. The security guard at the revolving door hardly paid any attention as he sought protection for himself from the rain under the doorway overhang. This was the last time anyone saw Lester Brandt.

Getting into Lester's apartment was no problem for Lou Silva. His specialty was breaking and entering and he had two prison terms to show for it. His assignment today was to remove several items from the apartment: a passport, any cash, any bank records, a small suitcase with several days of clothing, including a raincoat, and a toilet articles kit with a man's necessities. Any valuables would be taken as well. Silva knew the drill and carried it out like the true professional he was.

After two days' absence Lester's secretary called HR and reported his failure to answer her phone calls. The emergency number for him was his former wife's cell phone. The secretary called and Ivy promptly answered. She hadn't seen Lester for several weeks. She went over to his apartment to see if anything was amiss.

Her visit to his apartment didn't offer any reason for his disappearance. She knew where he kept his passport and was surprised to find it missing. She also saw his bathroom counter devoid of toiletries; another surprise. Ivy then called his attorney to learn if he had any information which would shed light on Lester's unexplained absence. He had nothing to offer except that Ivy was still listed in Lester's will as his sole beneficiary. If she had any questions about her ex's affairs in his absence, she should feel free to contact him.

CHAPTER 64

Perspiration dripped from her as the high-intensity program on her exercise cycle drew to a close. Leslie enjoyed the strenuous workout even though the room was only cooled by a fan.

The phone call from Ivy broke the mood. "Lester's gone AWOL, Leslie. No one has a clue where he might be. He vanished without a word to anyone. I think he skipped town for a reason known only to him. Anyway, I just called to share the news."

CHAPTER 65

Kate McCallister met Ivy in her office to go over a number of offers from major studios. Gail's letter not only dispelled the drug rumor but served to revive and heighten the studios' interest in Ivy.

Kate had gone through the offers in meticulous fashion so Ivy only had to hear Kate's presentation and indicate her enthusiasm or lack thereof. This process narrowed the options down to three and the two women were able to agree on a one-two-three ranking. The plan was for Kate to begin negotiating at the top of the list and then see if the one-two-three ranking changed after contract details were spelled out.

They broke for lunch at a nearby deli and an opportunity to revel in their good fortune. Kate couldn't contain her interest in Ivy's ability to get Gail Owens to capitulate so completely.

"Are you ready to share your magic formula for getting Gail to 'fess up, Ivy? It's a remarkable turnabout."

"You know, Kate, it's a bit of a blur to me. I mean it. You know how dreams dissolve? That's how I recall our meeting. I met Gail and I was able to get her to do the right thing. That's all I can tell you. I'm glad it worked out so well. As for details, I'm afraid I don't have any."

"Okay, Ivy, I can live with that. Guess I'll have to. On a different topic, *Love After Parting* has been nominated for a Golden Globe. The studio wants to celebrate so it's throwing a party for cast, production staff, and guests. You probably have the invitation on your messages. Check it. Pick a guest or two and enjoy yourself."

"You're my number one guest, Kate. You've brought me along to this point and I'm grateful. I think I'll ask Leslie to join us. Unfortunately, Doug's on the road in Atlanta."

CHAPTER 66

The Times featured Leslie's story on the front page, below the fold. John Livingstone couldn't have been more supportive. The managing editor was pleased to scoop *The Wall Street Journal* and gave Leslie high praise. Leslie was concerned about how much she left out. The focus was on the defective hip and the many patients in whom the device had been implanted. A second part dealt with how that came about; AllCare's pressure forcing the manufacturer to cut corners, then AllCare's failure, as well as the manufacturer's, to assure that the product hadn't been compromised. The latter drew upon Leslie's visit to Vietnam and her conversation with Tuan Bahn.

There was no mention of kickbacks and AllCare's monopoly position. This was on the advice of *the Times's* lawyers who felt pay-for-play had not been substantiated and could bring on blowback. Lester Brandt and Eric Dillon were two people caught in the spotlight. The orthopedists were treated more kindly.

For a follow-up piece, Leslie hoped to interview some patients.

There were so many words of congratulations from her peers, some in person and many over the phone, that Leslie almost missed Ivy's call inviting her to the studio party.

The party was held at Universal's Midtown office and studio in Manhattan, the same studio where Ivy had auditioned for her breakthrough role. The place was jammed with celebrants. The nomination was a great ego boost but winning could mean some unanticipated bonus money for the staff.

Leslie remembered a few of the staff from the cast party many months ago. Drink in hand she mingled freely. A faint tap on the shoulder got her to turn around and go face-to-face with a woman she remembered from the cast party but whose name eluded her. The woman was an attractive thirty-something with strong fumes of alcohol on her breath.

"Gail Owens, Ms. Newslady. I remember you as a friend of Ivy. I was a fellow cast member on *Love After Parting.*"

"Nice to meet you, Gail. Call me Leslie."

"I hear Ivy is getting offers from the big studios. Her part in *Love* really set her up. You know that part was originally going to be mine. I had to settle for a lesser role."

Leslie could tell from her slightly slurred speech and swaying posture that Gail was under the influence of several too many. Nevertheless, she was curious about what she had to say.

"I didn't know that. Tell me what happened?"

"You'd have to ask Ivy how she stole the part from me. Can't ask Jack Bauman." She hesitated a moment for her speech to catch up with her brain. "He's gone."

Kate McCallister joined them. "Hello, Gail. I see you're enjoying the studio's bar offerings."

"Anything wrong with that, Ms. Agent?"

"Not at all, Gail. Started any good rumors lately?"

"I can see Ivy sent her enforcer over here to intimidate me. I'm movin' on, ladies. Don't give her my regards." Gail turned away and melted into the crowd.

"What was that about, Kate; the rumor thing?"

"I'll give it to you in a nutshell. Ivy got the part in *Love After Parting* that Gail *thought* was hers. It hadn't been decided when they invited Ivy to audition. Ivy was innocent of *any* wrongdoing, but Gail held a grudge. She started a rumor that Ivy was a drug user and that effectively quashed any big studio offers. Somehow, Ivy got her to recant and that opened the floodgates for Ivy. I asked her how she got Gail to confess to the studios, but she was either evasive or unwilling to articulate how she did it. Very strange, but that's the story behind the rumor thing I chided the less-than-sober Gail about."

Leslie's curiosity was immediately aroused.

"Will you excuse me, Kate? I want to catch up with Gail and see if she has *any* recollection of her interaction with Ivy."

Leslie moved in the direction she last saw Gail headed. Her mind had switched onto the Jekyll and Hyde scenario for Ivy.

After searching through crowds in several rooms she spotted Gail leaning against a wall with an empty glass in her hand.

"Hey, Gail. I want to talk to you. Are you sober enough to recall your recent interaction with Ivy?"

"Yeah, I'm sober enough. She knocked me down when I let her into my apartment. She put a noose around my neck to choke me, nearly broke my arm and forced me to make copies of a letter she wrote. She was very threatening. Nothing like the person I worked with on the set of the movie. I was scared shitless. I didn't have any choice. I did what she told me to do. Anything to get her to leave me alone. That's it. I know the rumor I started was unfair, but she fucked her way into that part I was about to get."

"What do you mean?"

"I mean that the part was mine until she fucked Jack Bauman and he gave it to her."

"Okay. Thanks for giving me your side of the story, Gail. I needed to hear it."

"Yeah. I hope you never come face-to-face with that crazed bitch. She was scary."

Leslie turned and headed back to where she last saw Kate.

CHAPTER 67

Leslie left the party to get some fresh air. She took the elevator down and decided to walk a while. Gail's story had revived the Ivy Brandt story she'd been able to put aside while their friendship had blossomed. She had to share this with Diana.

Diana was finishing up work in her office when Leslie's call came through.

"Saw your story in the paper, Leslie. Quite a piece. Sad on so many fronts. Those poor people having to live with a bad hip after going through surgery and rehab. And the greed. Makes you wonder who you can trust."

"Thanks for your kind words, Diana. I called for a totally different reason. Our friend, Ivy, is uppermost on my mind."

Leslie related the entire Gail Owens story.

"Never got to talk to one of her purported victims 'til now. Cheryl Winter is gone and so is Jack Bauman. Gail Owens's story fits the Ivy profile and makes the other episodes seem plausible. Ivy needs help.

"I have to add a personal note here, Di. Ivy and I have become close. I'll tell you about this when we find some private time for serious talk. I just had to share this Gail Owens story with you. I heard it from Gail at a party an hour or so ago."

"I agree she needs help, Leslie, for her safety and the safety of others. Let's have lunch tomorrow. I'll call you in the morning with a time and location. I'm very busy but I'm sure I can break for lunch."

"I need your advice and sympathetic ear. Thanks again."

CHAPTER 68

Alyssa Ross sipped her breakfast coffee with *The New York Times* propped up in front of her on a tabletop easel. Her penthouse condo was bathed in bright morning sunlight. Luke Rollins sat opposite her reading the sports section.

Morning coffee time was a weekly meeting at which Rollins updated Alyssa on any matters requiring her attention. This morning Alyssa was the one doing the update. "Put down the paper, Luke. I just finished Leslie Nugent's article on the hip joint matter. Looks like she chose not to mention the payola issue we were so concerned about. Maybe that storm cloud has blown over."

Luke was less sanguine. "Maybe. Or possibly she doesn't have enough solid information to raise the question in print. Yet. I'd keep an eye on her before thinking we lucked out."

"You're probably right, Luke. Stay on her a bit longer and see if she's still sniffing around that angle. If she has a suspicion, she's likely to keep after it. At least for now we can take a breather.

CHAPTER 69

It was one of Doug's free nights while in the city. The playoff schedule had several open days so he and Ivy made good use of the time. Tonight, they were relaxing with Leslie and Brad in the latter's apartment. They had brought in food from a Midtown restaurant that specialized in "soup-to-nuts" take-out meals.

Doug raised his glass and offered a toast. "To a wild and crazy couple who have decided to cohabitate. To us, Doug and Ivy." The glasses clinked.

Leslie gave Ivy a curious look. "When did you decide to do this?"

"Doug sprung the idea tonight when he came to pick me up. I guess he thought he'd take me by surprise, and he did. We've agreed to give it a try and see if it works. Doug'll move in with me after the playoffs and still maintain his apartment in case my housekeeping style is too dysfunctional for him."

Brad offered a second toast. "To Doug and Ivy, a *not* wild and crazy couple. Good luck." The glasses clinked again.

CHAPTER 70

Ivy and Leslie sat next to each other on a bench in Central Park. The fall foliage was peaking and was a definite attraction.

"Les, I was thinking about buying a house north of the city. It would be a retreat; a place I could go to whenever life in the city gets too intense for me. Sure, it would be vacant much of the time if my filming took me to some faraway place. But it would be there when it was needed."

"I assume you're talking a pretty piece of change, Ivy. Would Doug be partnering with you on the financing?"

"We haven't talked about it, but I think I can carry it on my own. My divorce was more financially advantageous than I had any reason to expect."

"Spell that out for me, Ivy. I'm interested."

"Well, Lester had a hoard of money in some Caribbean bank, I think it's called Cayman International. He never told me about it. I gave Diana ten thousand dollars to squeeze some crucial info out of a Cayman employee. She had her investigator go down there and find a malleable VP. He found one. I remember his odd name, Mason Lord. The rest is history. I received a large share of the stash, about four point five million."

"So that means he probably had twice that, Ivy, somewhere near nine million. Did you have an inkling that he'd squirreled away so much money?"

"No way. We lived well on his salary but there was little left over at the end of the month, or so I thought."

"So. Where'd he get nine million dollars?"

"I have no idea, Les, and Diana told me not to get interested in that question. For tax reasons my ignorance works in my favor."

Leslie had no trouble putting two and two together. Clay Webster had spelled out the scenario for her. You buy the guy who makes the big purchasing decisions and that's your ticket. Ivy was sitting on a piece of those ill-gotten gains and her lawyer had told her to remain dumb as a broom about the origin of the money. Lester was gone, who knows where, but Eric Dillon was still around. For Leslie, her gunsight was trained on Eric Dillon with the certainty that he was paymaster in a payola scheme.

CHAPTER 71

Sitting in Alyssa's office, they could see the sun's fireball setting across the Hudson River. The troika of Luke Rollins, Marjorie Bannister, and Alyssa Ross was the brain trust aiming to keep the payola problem from seeing the light of day.

Luke had a broad smile on his face as he spoke. "The listening device I planted in Nugent's apartment finally paid off, Alyssa. The reporter is trying to dig into the payola matter. She doesn't have any hard facts, but she has the scent. I don't know where she's going with it but I'm sure she's gonna keep digging."

"Great work, Luke. I see two possible paths of action. First, we let the reporter spin her wheels chasing evidence that doesn't exist, or secondly, we convince her that it's in her own self-interest to just let it rest. Trouble with even a veiled threat is that it implies there's something valuable someone wants to hide. That's catnip to a reporter."

The two women turned toward Luke. Alyssa took the lead. "Luke, we want your opinion. Which strategy works for you?"

Luke didn't hesitate. "I guess I'd go with a simple request that she back off. It could start as a request but have the overtone of a serious threat."

Alyssa flashed a smile.

"Okay. How do we deliver the message? Does one of us do it face-to-face? If so, who is the messenger?"

"I think Luke should do it. I'd keep you out of it, Alyssa. If she proves unwilling to back off, you may have to come forward and use your powers of persuasion."

"Works for me, guys. A soft touch to start out."

CHAPTER 72

News from Kate McCallister couldn't have been more positive. Her negotiations with Allied Studios, their first choice among the offers, had gone very well. She was trying for a few perks but considered it a done deal without the perks. Next step was for Ivy to hear the details of the offer. They set up a meeting in Kate's office for the very next day.

The news was too good for Ivy to keep to herself, so she called Leslie at work. Leslie's workday was going to end late, so she suggested they meet at her reporter's cubicle in *the Times* building. Leslie would be at a meeting but would return to her space around seven.

Sitting in the cubicle, Ivy took in the aroma and buzz of a still busy early evening newspaper work area. Leslie's phone was on her desk with a note underneath it telling Ivy to make herself comfortable and check out some preliminary stories she'd printed out for her.

The phone rang and Ivy could see a name in caller ID she didn't recognize. She decided to answer the phone in case it was a call Leslie wouldn't want to miss.

"Leslie Nugent, here."

"Glad I got you Ms. Nugent. I have some information about the AllCare-Metro situation which might interest you. I was hoping we could meet and let me deliver the message face-to-face. I'm very near *the Times* building."

Ivy was unsure what to do but decided to keep the conversation going.

"Okay, how about meeting in the lobby of *the Times* building in ten minutes. I'm sure we can find a quiet space to sit and talk."

"Sounds great. I'll be there in ten."

Ivy was unsure if this was a good move but she chose to play it out. She penned a brief note for Leslie and left it under the phone.

Luke Rollins had never seen either Leslie Nugent or Ivy Brandt. He assumed the woman loitering in the lobby was the reporter.

"I'm here to deliver a message, Ms. Nugent."

Ivy quickly understood his mistake in identifying her as Leslie but chose not to correct the misidentification. She was curious to hear the message this stranger was going to deliver to Leslie.

Ivy spotted a bench against a wall in the spacious lobby and led the stranger over to it.

"I wanted the message to be delivered as clearly as possible and I thought doing it in person would be the most effective way.

"Okay. I'm all ears."

"Here's the message. Your interest in the relationship between AllCare and Metro Hospital is bothersome for my employer. Said employer would like you to back off from that line of investigation. It's a *personal* matter so said employer would be most appreciative. Trust me, my employer *really* cares about this and would be very disappointed by your rejection of this simple request."

The actress remained outwardly calm and composed even though a threat was implied. Her internal alarm system was turned on, not that Luke could notice any change in her demeanor.

"So, it's an exchange; I placate your employer and your employer doesn't mess with me. Is that it?"

"Exactly. It's not a financial deal. We just exchange comfort measures. I'm leaving you a card with my cell phone number. I'll expect your call in forty-eight hours, hopefully indicating that you found the offer reasonable. My employer likes to keep it simple."

Ivy and Leslie had never discussed Leslie's involvement in any AllCare-Metro interaction. Nevertheless, she could appreciate an element of danger for Leslie in the stranger's presentation.

She rose from the bench and Luke did likewise, acknowledging that the meeting was over. She maintained her composure and delivered a rejoinder to his message.

"I don't take kindly to threats, Mr. Whoever. If your employer is bothered by my interest in AllCare's relationship with Metro, we can discuss the matter. That such interest requires your heavy-handed approach makes me think there's something worth investigating."

As he turned to leave, she called to him. "I'll be sure to pass along your message to Leslie Nugent when she gets here."

Twenty minutes later Leslie found her friend relaxing in her cubicle.

"Aren't you the contented one, Ivy? I'll just need a few minutes to check my phone for messages and make a few notes based on the meeting I just attended."

"No rush, Les. Before we go though, let me tell you about a call you had and the stranger I met in place of you not half an hour ago."

Leslie sat before her computer and briefly typed some notes for herself. She next turned to Ivy and asked her to resume her odd tale.

"A stranger called and I represented myself as you. We met in the lobby downstairs and he delivered a message from his employer whom he never identified by name or sex. The message was simple: you stop looking into the relationship between AllCare and Metro and in exchange that employer will be most grateful. He was subtle about the or-else threat relating to you but it was implied. That about sums it up."

Leslie was trying to take it all in. Her mind was racing, trying to determine who was sufficiently bothered by her investigation to go so far as to threaten her, albeit in a subtle manner.

"I guess there's something someone wants me to keep quiet about AllCare and Metro. This only confirms my suspicion that something is not wholesome about the relationship."

"That's what I told the guy."

"What else did you tell him?"

"That I, or rather you, didn't like being threatened. I, or rather you, found it offensive. That's it. He left. Oh, yes, I suggested his employer talk to you about the matter if it bothers him or her so much."

"Is that all, Ivy?"

"Best as I can recollect."

"This is a real-life thriller we're acting in. What do you think the next step would be?"

"Just sit tight and wait for a call from the employer inviting you to come and have a discussion."

"That's just what I had in mind to do."

Leslie was surprised how calm she was. She might have been prepared to let the AllCare-Metro story end with the piece she already had in print. But, no. There was more ore to be mined there. Her reporter's instinct wouldn't let go of this.

CHAPTER 73

The two women were deep into a plate of meze when the anticipated call came. Leslie's phone said the caller was Marjorie Bannister, a person not known to Leslie. Her guess was that it was an invitation to powwow about the matter Ivy had reported to Leslie. She accepted the call.

"Is this Leslie Nugent?"

"Yes, it is. How can I help you?"

"I'm Marjorie Bannister, a colleague of the person who'd like to meet with you. She'd like you to come to a meeting tomorrow at one. I expect you know the reason for the meeting."

"I do and I will."

"Good. I'm going to text you the location. I expect you to come alone."

"Okay. See you at one." The call ended.

"As I'm sure you guessed, Ivy, that was an invitation to meet and discuss the issue, as you suggested to the messenger this afternoon."

"Will follow with interest, Leslie."

CHAPTER 74

The offices of Ross-Wagner had a certain charm. They occupied the two top floors in a lower Manhattan classic early twentieth century ten-story building. The building, owned by Ross-Wagner, had resisted updates to make it contemporary. Rather, the owner had invested in maintaining its century-old style. It had class.

Leslie found her way to Marjorie Bannister's office and was greeted by a secretary seated in an entry alcove.

"I know you're Leslie Nugent. The entry desk called ahead of you. Thank you for being on time. You can go right in."

The secretary opened the office door and ushered Leslie into a large office decorated in classic 1930 style. Leslie found it impressive in its conservative decor. A slender Marjorie Bannister was standing near the large picture window that looked out on the tip of Manhattan. She wore a knee-length, sleeveless black wool dress with a high neckline. Short gray hair framed an attractive face.

She turned to greet her visitor. "I'm Marge and you're Leslie, if that's okay with you."

"Certainly, Marge."

"I'm sure you know what the meeting is about. I'm the executive vice president of Ross-Wagner. You'll be meeting with Alyssa Ross, the company president and owner. Her office is right next door to mine. I'm not going to attend the meeting. It's a personal matter so Alyssa will keep it private.

I'm here to put you at ease. There'll be coffee in Alyssa's office or tea if you prefer. Is there anything you'd like to ask me?"

"Well, maybe one thing. Why did you feel it necessary to threaten me before even having a conversation?"

"It is a bit heavy-handed, I grant you. I hope we'll get past that."

"I'm not sure we can since the threat is already out there."

"As I said, I hope we'll get past that. At least, as best we can. I think you'll find Alyssa a very understanding person. Now let me introduce you. We can go in through this connecting door."

Marjorie showed Leslie into an adjoining office of similar size and decor. Alyssa Ross greeted her with a smile and a handshake. Alyssa, like Marge, was a woman in her fifties, dressed elegantly in a man-tailored dark gray suit. Her hair was grey, like Marge's, straight and shoulder-length. She was an appealing woman who looked every bit the formidable executive of a large international company.

"Thank you for coming, Leslie. Help yourself to tea or coffee on the table."

The women each chose a cup of coffee. Alyssa motioned to Leslie to take one of the chairs facing the window.

"I find myself in the uncomfortable position of wanting to influence a reporter's instinctive need to follow a scent no matter where it leads, in this case your interest in the relationship between AllCare and Metro Hospitals." She held up a hand just as Leslie was about to respond.

"Let me continue. Eric Dillon is my son-in-law. AllCare was a wedding gift from me to my daughter and her husband. He built it into a major company, but his ego has tripped him up, leading to that unfortunate hip joint tragedy. *How* he built the company is another story and that's where I'd like you to let go of the bone you've got your teeth into. A scandal over unspecified matters would hurt my daughter and that's why I'm talking to you. It's *personal* for me."

"I appreciate that background, Alyssa. However, I'm more than a little miffed by the threat your messenger laid out mistakenly for my friend. You haven't gotten to that part of your pitch but I'm sure it'll come up when you turn the page on this request you laid out as an opener."

"Would you have been willing to even conditionally accommodate me if that threat wasn't hanging over you? I doubt it. I'm taking that off the table as best I can and repeating my request that you stop at the water's edge with your investigation."

"You may be well-intentioned now that you threatened me. If I go along with your request, it'll *look* like I capitulated under the pressure you say is no longer being exerted. Just granting your request for a personal favor *without* any pressure would imply we have a relationship that doesn't exist. As a reporter I'd be giving up a potentially juicy story that I already have begun to flesh out. Nevertheless, I will consider your request. Let's leave it at that for the moment."

"Okay, Leslie. But please get back to me with a definitive answer once you settle on one. There I am, making another request."

"Okay, Alyssa. I will. Don't know why I should trust you given our situation."

The meeting ended with a handshake. Leslie was escorted out of the building and into a waiting limousine with the driver instructed to take her wherever she wanted to go.

CHAPTER 75

Leslie needed to talk to someone about her dilemma. If she couldn't talk to Brad that would be a bad omen for their deepening relationship.

He answered his cell phone on the third ring. "Leslie, I'm with a client but I want to see you, so how about that rib place we ate in a few weeks ago? See you there at seven thirty? Just say okay."

"Okay."

She didn't have enough time to go home and freshen up so she headed over to the restaurant to have a drink while she waited for Brad. Sitting at the bar in the bustling restaurant, she wondered how many of her fellow drinkers were facing a thorny decision. It seemed her life was more complicated than it should be. A great job and a super guy should be the formula for happiness. She hoped Brad would help her work her way out of the thicket. Leslie was almost ready to order a second margarita when Brad put his arms around her from behind.

"Order yours and one for me. Whatever you're having is what I want."

She turned on her barstool and kissed him firmly on the lips.

"Now that's the way I like to be greeted," he said. "Passion, pure and simple."

She leaned back to look at him. No question, he brightened her mood.

"Let's get to our table, Les," he suggested. "You have an expectant look, so I suspect there's something on your mind you want to tell me."

The wait for their table was mercifully short as they watched tray after tray of juicy ribs parade by them. They carried their drinks to the table. Once seated, Leslie started right in.

"Brad, there's something on my mind so I'll get right to it. I'm pursuing a story that seems to have hit the nerve of a dangerous person. That person is powerful and has threatened me if I don't drop the story I'm pursuing. Although she—and it is a woman—framed her request as a simple personal appeal I think there's more to it than that.

"Years ago, I defied her when I was pursuing a different story. Fortunately, the matter was resolved before I got in too deep and drew her fire. But here's the twist. The guy I was seeing tried to get me to back off the story because it was dangerous. I didn't take his advice and he took that as a sign I placed my job ahead of my private life. We parted company.

"I'm at that same fork in the road again but now I place my private life above my job. I don't want to lose you over *any* story."

Brad didn't hesitate to respond. "Leslie, of course I don't want to see you place yourself in a dangerous position. On the other hand, I know your job has that potential. It's the price you pay for being a good reporter. If you were an astronaut or a fighter pilot I wouldn't insist that you quit your chosen profession. I love you and trust you to know when it's time to be extra cautious."

Leslie reached across the table and kissed him. "I needed to hear that, Brad."

CHAPTER 76

Leads in the AllCare story had dried up. This allowed Leslie to focus on an unrelated matter: Ivy's bizarre dual personality. It haunted her. Ivy was a genuine friend but her propensity for violence kept Leslie from feeling comfortable when she contemplated the two of them being alone in a private setting. She knew her concern wasn't fully justified, but it existed nonetheless. In the interest of their friendship, she'd planned to discuss Ivy's condition with a psychiatrist.

Janice Allen was a longtime friend of Leslie's mother. She served as an occasional consultant for Leslie when psychiatric issues needed clarification in an evolving story. Although a private practice psychiatrist, she was well-respected in the academic community as evidenced by her mentoring role in the psychiatric residency at Columbia.

Allen always made time for her friend's daughter at the end of her office hours. She looked forward to the interesting challenges Leslie's questions brought up.

The Park Avenue office was finally empty and Allen welcomed Leslie into her consultation room. They sat facing each other in twin easy chairs.

Leslie thanked Janice for making time for her and then spelled out why she was there. She related Ivy's past history and her concern about a dual personality. Ivy's role in Cheryl Winter's and Jack Bauman's deaths was pure conjecture but the incident with Gail Owens was real. The tale Diana related from college was credible in the context of these other events.

"Leslie, I understand where you're heading. Psychiatry recognizes an entity labeled 'dissociative identity disorder' but many in the field do not accept DID as a credible psychiatric entity. Having said this by way of an introduction let me cut to the chase. Your friend may well have a disorder with features of DID.

"We don't know if she was traumatized emotionally as a child or adolescent but this could serve as the basis for her problem. Incest is but one trauma often lurking in the background. Her amnesia for past violent events fits the pattern. The stress trigger for the incidents that concern you seems consistent and may represent some form of betrayal or attempted control over her.

"Rather than focus on giving her problem a proper name I would instead agree that there is a serious problem that needs attention. I wouldn't be surprised if she *didn't* overtly display evidence of the problem for a long period of time. She may seem perfectly normal if she doesn't encounter any triggers in her life."

Allen paused and looked at Leslie for a response.

"Thanks, Jan. That's helpful. It lends credence to my concern that there is a real problem here. Her manifestation of the disorder may very well be peculiar to *her*. Now, how do I get her to accept that she *has* a problem and needs therapy? All I want to do is get her into the hands of a professional to whom she will relate."

"Leslie, don't expect thanks from her when you tell her she needs help. She may question your friendship. She probably doesn't have a clear recollection of the incidents you cited. All you can do is lean heavily on your friendship and ask her to trust you. Don't give up if you meet resistance and even hostility."

The following day, Leslie was meeting Ivy for lunch just

outside Central Park. Ivy's serious problem was on Leslie's agenda for the lunch hour. Lacking a vivid memory of the violence would make it difficult to get her to accept her disordered behavior. All Leslie was hoping for was Ivy's acquiescence that she had a problem and might benefit from some kind of therapeutic intervention; a foot in the door.

The food trucks alongside the park offered a variety of international cuisine. They carried their trays into the park and found an empty bench. Ivy was on alert. She sensed Leslie had an agenda. She could tell from her face that there was a serious matter she wanted to discuss.

"Okay, Les, let's dive in. I can tell you're champing at the bit."

"Bear with me, Ivy. I wonder if you're aware of your propensity to resort to violent action when facing a critical challenge. I'm speaking as your dearest friend. I only have a few episodes secondhand but there's enough to make a case that you should seek help."

"I'm not sure what you're talking about, Les. You'll have to be more explicit." Leslie could sense Ivy turning cold.

"Okay. I spoke to Gail Owens at the recent studio party. She related an episode in which you terrorized her into recanting her vicious rumor. She said she was scared shitless. Those were her exact words. The way she recalled the incident was very convincing. There are other examples that I'm less conversant with, but they fit the pattern. Does any of this ring a bell, Ivy?"

"No, Leslie. I'm afraid you've been fed some scurrilous tales about me that *shouldn't* ring true to *you*. I'm surprised you put any stock in them."

Leslie could see Ivy's defenses were fully engaged. Her denial was going to make it difficult to penetrate her protective wall.

"Ivy, let's get this straight. You're a dear friend and I only know you as a delightful, witty and charming person. Those incidents took place outside the boundary of our relationship. That you don't recall them is part of the problem. Please bear with me. You need help even though you can't see the problem. *That*'s the problem a professional would work through with you, but you have to give me the benefit of a doubt."

"I'm stunned by what you've told me, Leslie. I don't agree with your assessment of my personality. But, in the interest of our relationship and in all fairness to Doug, I'll go along with what you're going to suggest. At least for a while."

"That's a start, Ivy. I'll get back to you with the name of a person who I think you'll be comfortable with. I'm glad we talked and you're willing to at least take the first step."

CHAPTER 77

Leslie thought back in time to a story she had been dog-gedly pursuing that led a guy very close to her to dissolve their romance. He'd felt her willingness to court danger, in spite of his wish that she stand down, reflected poorly on their relationship. She recalled meeting a friend of his who helped her unravel the story's mystery. Both men alluded to a high-level person who was, in the friend's words, "not to be messed with."

In retrospect, as she recalled the earlier story, Leslie now believed that Alyssa Ross very likely was that person not to be messed with. This time around, her decision to pursue a story would again have to be made in the context of Alyssa's strong personal wish that Leslie cease and desist.

Rather than drop a good story, Leslie decided to pitch it to a friend in the Manhattan DA's office to determine if there was a case they might pursue. If the answer was a solid no, she'd drop it. No sense banging her head against a wall and incurring the wrath of Alyssa Ross.

CHAPTER 78

Leslie met Patricia Coleman in her downtown office. Leslie and Pat were longtime friends from college days. Pat had been with the district attorney's office for several years as an assistant DA and was always ready to help her old schoolmate sort out some complex legal matter.

"Hey, Pat. Thanks for giving me some of your valuable time."

"I always enjoy helping you out, Leslie. The problems you bring in here are usually complicated and frustrating, just my meat."

"Today won't be an exception. I want you to hear what I know and tell me if I'm spinning my wheels to no useful end. I'll be brief."

"I'm all ears. Fire away."

Leslie related the story.

"The vice president for purchasing at Metro Hospital Systems was having an adulterous affair. His mistress had a strong suspicion that her lover had a secret stash of money at a bank in the Caribbean. She was going to pass that information to the VP's wife who was taking steps to divorce her husband. Her hope was that she'd negotiate for a share of the divorce settlement. The mistress abruptly disappeared but not before the wife got some info about the stash. Much later it was determined that the mistress was murdered and cremated. The wife had no knowledge about the source of the money but received a significant portion of it in the divorce settlement. Okay so far?"

"I'm fine, Leslie. Keep going."

"My snooping led me to understand that AllCare, the medical supply company servicing Metro, had a virtual monopoly. A very lucrative monopoly. I was led to understand that such monopoly situations are not unusual in the industry and often are the result of the supply company buying off the VP for purchasing."

"I'm getting the gist of your story, Leslie. You suspect the VP's stash is a result of his relationship with AllCare. It's called a kickback and in this instance is also a bribe."

"Let me go on. The VP suddenly goes missing. To this day, no one knows where or why. The AllCare CEO stonewalled me when I interviewed him about a tragic medical device problem looming large over Metro and AllCare. He's certainly not going to come clean about the kickbacks." Leslie paused here, reached into her shoulder bag, and produced a three-page document. "Here's a copy of the article I just published in *the Times* about the device failure."

"Okay, Leslie. Two bodies, one cremated and one not found. Bribery and kickbacks suspect but no recipient to question. Cash stashed away but no lead to the source."

"There's more, Pat. Stay with me. A small food supply company threatening to raise a ruckus about the AllCare monopoly has now quieted down after finally being given a piece of the Metro food business. Coincidence?"

"Is there more?"

"Last piece. The mother-in-law of the AllCare CEO does not want her daughter tarnished by a bribery/kickback scandal. She wants me to drop my investigative reporting and move on to something else. I think that's about it."

"Okay, Leslie. It's an interesting story and may be just

as you presented it. The whistleblower girlfriend is gone. The payee in your kickback scheme is gone. The monopoly purchased with the bribe is no longer in effect. That leaves the briber. His lawyer will keep his client's lips buttoned up. Sounds like the mother-in-law had good advice for you. Two possible murders to keep the situation quiet suggests someone really means business. I think you'd have a hard time digging up any useful information to strengthen your case. It's intriguing but intrigue often leads nowhere."

"You're suggesting I let it rest. And that's my inclination, only because I have no leads to follow at this time."

Leslie chose not to call Alyssa and tell her she was backing off. She wasn't actively pursuing the story but was keeping an open file on her desk. You never know.

CHAPTER 79

TWO MONTHS LATER

"Hey, Ivy, I'd like to run an idea by you. I know you just finished filming *A Dying Passion* so I wondered if our foursome might sneak away for a week of sun and relaxation on an island somewhere. St. Thomas? St. Barts? Grand Cayman? What do you think?"

Ivy put her phone on speaker so Doug could listen in.

"Doug's listening in on speakerphone, Leslie. We think it's a great idea. Why don't you let me put my travel agent on it? She gets a lot of business from me and will work her fingers to the bone to keep me happy. Doug's nodding his approval. The offseason is great travel time for him. He says he stayed at a very private beachfront resort on Grand Cayman and liked the island."

"Okay, Ivy. Get your agent moving on this. I'm thinking sometime in January or early February, just two months from now. Brad's on board. He's gonna cover our share of the resort expense. I discussed it with him before I called you."

"I'm already starting to pack, Les. My next shoot doesn't begin until April and Doug goes to spring training in mid-February, so I'm looking forward to sun and fun to fill the days. I'll call as soon as I hear from my travel agent."

"Before we hang up, Ivy, there's something else I want to say. First, turn off the speakerphone. This is just between the two of us. I know we've both avoided any mention of the topic I laid on you several months ago. I don't know if you pursued the psychiatrist I recommended. I've kept out of that aspect of your life. Now, I'm just itching to know how, or if, it's working out. Anything you're willing to share would be welcome. I'm not looking for any details, just the smallest overview."

"Leslie, I hear you. I'll share some thoughts with you. The woman you recommended is special. I can't thank you enough. I meet with her twice a week and something is happening that I never expected: she has me reliving my past and facing some painful memories. I'm digging deep into myself and gaining an insight I desperately needed. I don't know how far we'll get but I know I'm ready for whatever is coming. I'm beginning to understand why you were so persistent. I'll stop here."

"Thanks, Ivy. That's reassuring. I'm glad it seems to be a worthwhile venture."

The travel agent didn't waste any time putting a proposal in front of Ivy.

"Sand Cove on Grand Cayman is a great spot. It's an adult resort and attracts people looking for a tranquil paradise. Food is excellent and accommodations are first-class.

"It's pricey but not outrageous. I'm emailing you the brochures right now so you can see what it looks like and what it offers in terms of recreation. If it's a go, give me a call and I'll arrange the dates and transportation."

It *was* a go and six weeks later the foursome flew down first class.

They settled into their two-bedroom cottage and enjoyed the private pool. The ocean beach was only a few dozen yards from their patio.

On their third day they rented a jeep and drove into Georgetown, the capital, for a shopping excursion.

The stroll down the main drag was one duty-free store after another. Ivy picked up a few bikini bathing suits and a wide brimmed straw hat. Leslie, on a modest budget, limited herself to one bikini.

Leslie's eye caught a sign over a nondescript building on the main street: Cayman International Bank. A bell rang in her head.

She huddled with Ivy in a small sandal shop.

"Ivy, would you lend me some money, say ten thousand dollars? Right now?"

"Sure, Leslie. No problem. I keep a large balance in my money market account. Gonna tell me what it's for?"

"I think this is the bank where Lester buried his treasure. I want to see if I can find that VP you told me about who had information for sale. You told me his odd name; do you recall it?"

Ivy looked skyward for a moment and then blurted out, "Mason Lord. It's a name I can't forget."

"Great. All I want to know is how the money got here. Just the name of the sender will do. I think some money will pry that info out of the bank's records. I hope my paper will reimburse me, seeing this as a business expense. It's a gamble but one I need to take. I'm gonna call my editor and see if he gives me the go-ahead."

"You're going to do that right now?"

"Yep. But first, you have to go in and have your bank wire ten K to this bank and have them hand you the cash in exchange for some outrageous bank fee. Then you hand me the cash. Okay?"

"Sounds like a plan to me. Wait here while this actress goes in and acts out a small talking part."

The return call to Leslie from New York gave her a green

light, though she detected a slight tremble in John Livingstone's voice.

Half an hour later Ivy emerged smiling and handed Leslie an envelope stuffed with large bills.

"Go for it, girl. I'll find the guys and keep them busy."

CHAPTER 80

The bank was drab on the outside, but the interior would make any bank in the US proud. The vaulted ceiling and painted walls were bright and well cared for. Leslie had to decide which employee to approach.

The decision was made for her when a youngish male in a well-tailored navy suit came forward and welcomed her to Cayman International.

"I'm Mason Lord, vice president for customer service. How can I be of help to you?"

Leslie smiled to herself about the lucky coincidence of meeting the very VP she had hoped to find. He seemed self-assured and, despite his seeming youth, gave the impression of being competent.

"I'm Leslie Nugent. I'm looking for information about an account at the bank. The account is under the name Lester Brandt."

"Well, Ms. Nugent, our accounts are very confidential so there's very limited information I can pass on to you. Perhaps if you tell me what you wish to know I can offer some assistance."

"Thank you, Mr. Lord. All I'm seeking is the name of the person or persons who have deposited money into the account. And possibly some data about the sender or senders."

"Hmm. That's a bit tricky. Can you provide me with some of your identification papers? That would help."

Leslie took the envelope Ivy had given her and handed it to Mr. Lord. It contained half of Ivy's cash. She was holding the other half in reserve.

Lord looked at it briefly and excused himself to "examine it more closely."

"I'll be right back, Ms. Nugent." He went into one of the interview rooms nearby after leading Leslie to a comfortable chair in the spacious lobby.

Counting the bills, Leslie assumed. She sat patiently. Lord didn't take long to count the money in the envelope. He emerged with a straight face and continued the charade.

"I think I need some more identification papers, Ms. Nugent. The ones you provided are in order but there is a need for more documents."

"I have a few more. If you give me a moment, I'll find them in my backpack." Leslie reached into her pack and found the remaining five K. She asked for an envelope which Lord graciously provided. She put the money in it and handed it to Lord. He then returned briefly to the interview room and reemerged a few minutes later with a satisfied smile on his face.

"I think you have the necessary documents, Ms. Nugent. If you'll be patient, I'll need some time to obtain the information you requested. It may take me fifteen minutes or so."

Leslie smiled and indicated with a turn of her hand that she'd give him all the time he needed. He left, disappearing into the back of the bank where highly confidential information was stored which could be accessed for a considerable price.

Ten minutes later he returned with a folder containing a single sheet of paper. He handed it to her for inspection. No words were exchanged. Leslie looked the sheet of paper over and confirmed that it contained the information she was looking for. She and Lord shook hands and he accompanied her to the bank's exit.

Out in the sunny street, Ivy was leaning against a shaded wall.

"Get what you were after?"

"I think so. It cost that whole wad of cash. I hope it'll be worth it. My paper may find the price a bit high to swallow."

Back at the cottage Leslie had an opportunity to inspect her prize in some detail. The same person made wire transfers each month. The name was not one that Leslie recognized. In each case the money was transferred from the US bank to Cayman International using an international money transferring service. There was no apparent business associated with the money transferred; i.e., no goods or services were exchanged for the money. The IRS reporting requirement might not be met.

Leslie and Ivy joined the men on the patio of their cottage and enjoyed the late sunset. Leslie's pursuit of the story would have to wait until she returned to the States. She believed the new information put her back in the hunt for a big payola story.

Alyssa's eventual reaction would have to be reckoned with.

CHAPTER 81

A blind ad in the local newspaper had attracted Paul Gemma's attention. His hardware store was doing a modest business in the north Bronx, but Amazon and other big mail-order companies were beginning to gnaw away at his margin. The big-box stores were the other predators. The ad said the opportunity was unusual; make some money with no risk and little effort. He called the phone number in the ad. After an interview with a man who never identified himself, he signed on for the job.

The requirements were simple: open a new Chase bank account, pick up cash when called, deposit the cash in the new account, and wire transfer it using a prescribed international money transfer service to a designated bank account in Cayman International. For each pickup and transfer he would be paid $500 in cash when the transaction was completed. His payment would be at a prearranged drop much the same as the pickup for transfer.

Gemma never saw any people carry out the transactions, and he had no number to call with questions. When he signed on, he was given a not-so-subtle warning to play it straight or face the consequences. The money was good, and the warning seemed genuine.

Paul Gemma was the name Leslie gleaned from the paper Mason Lord had given her in exchange for $10,000. Gemma was the bagman in the AllCare kickback scheme. With Lester Brandt gone the cash cow was out of milk.

CHAPTER 82

Hardware Depot wasn't difficult to find in the Bronx. It was a throwback to the fifties, stubbornly surviving in a highly competitive world. Inside the store the customer was closely surrounded by floor to ceiling hardware devices, some in boxes, many just displayed openly on shelves or wall hangers. It looked like chaos. Leslie wondered how, if ever, inventory was taken.

A smiling clerk wearing a denim apron approached her and asked if he could help her.

"Maybe. I'm looking for Paul Gemma."

The smile faded and was replaced by a poker face.

"I'm Paul. What can I do for you?"

"I think the matter I want to discuss would best be handled in private. Is there some place we can go to have a conversation?"

Gemma remained poker-faced. He was confronted by a woman he'd never seen before and was suspicious she was from some law enforcement agency.

"Possibly. Who are you and what do you want?"

"I'm Leslie Nugent. A reporter with *The New York Times*."

She handed him her business card. He scanned it and handed it back.

"I'm no threat to you, Mr. Gemma. I just want some information."

Gemma motioned her to follow him as he headed toward

the back of the store. They entered a small office cluttered with hardware. He shut the door and cleared a seat for her to sit down.

"I'll get right to the point, Mr. Gemma. I know you've been wiring money to a bank in Grand Cayman for a number of years. I suspect you're just a conduit in a larger scheme. All I'm after is the name of the person you do this work for. That's all. I have no interest in getting you in trouble with the IRS or any authority that deals with illegal money transfers. I just want to trace the money back to its source."

Gemma remained on high alert but was willing to cooperate since he knew so little.

"I do the money transfer, but I never see another person. It's all done by phone and simple money drops. I have no idea what's going on. I just pick up the money and do the transfer. I get five hundred dollars for each transfer. That, too, is through a prearranged drop. That's it. Now you know everything."

Leslie sat quietly. She had thought this scenario through beforehand so she was prepared with a follow-up question.

"I'm sure you met someone when you signed on. He or she had to explain the routine and also convince you not to think about skimming any money. Do you remember that person?"

"It was years ago, and he never used a name. Sorry."

"If I sent an artist over, could you try to recall his face and help recreate his likeness? That might help. That's all I'd ask. Do your best."

"I'll try."

"The artist will come to the store in a day or two. I appreciate your cooperation."

Two days later Gemma sat with a police artist who was

doing Chan Young a favor. After an hour of work, Gemma felt he'd done all he could with a faded memory. He felt the image was a reasonable approximation of the man he'd met almost ten years ago.

Leslie now had an image to work with but no name to go with it.

CHAPTER 83

Spring training for the baseball season was winding down. Ivy had spent several weeks in March with Doug in Florida but was now back up north, preparing for a new film to be shot in New York City. Wardrobe fittings, script readings, regular workouts, and dialect coaching consumed her days. Tonight, she, Leslie, and Brad were heading to Lincoln Center where they had tickets to the New York Philharmonic. Ivy and Brad had come over to Leslie's apartment for deli sandwiches before they headed over to the concert.

Humming away in the kitchen, Ivy unwrapped the sandwiches and set them on a large plate on the kitchen table along with three cans of diet soda. She was clearing papers from the table when she noticed an artist's charcoal portrait among the papers.

"Hey, Leslie, get in here," she called from the kitchen.

Leslie came in, drying her hair with a towel.

"Okay, Ivy, what's up?"

Ivy pointed at the picture on the table.

"I know this guy, Les. He's the guy I met in place of you in *the Times* building and heard the threat. Yep, that's the guy. Whoever drew this is pretty good."

Leslie was stunned. Ivy noted her shocked expression.

"How'd you get this picture, Les? Why do you have it?"

"I'll explain it all to you in a moment. Recognizing the guy in that picture has set my mind running at top speed. I want you to hear my recent take on the news story that guy was sent to suppress. Just listen.

"When we were down in Grand Cayman, you remember, I went into a bank on the hunch that it was the bank Lester used to sequester his money. I was right. That's where your fat settlement came from. That ten K I borrowed from you bought me the name of the guy who made the money transfers into the account. Are you following me?"

"I am indeed. Sounds like you made good use of my money."

"The guy couldn't provide a name but was able, with the assistance of a police sketch artist, to identify from memory the man who recruited him years ago. You just added crucial confirmation of the guy's identity. That same guy was obviously sent to threaten me if I didn't stop work on a story his boss wanted me to shelve. Are you still following me?"

"I get it. Now you've connected that message boy with the payola scheme. I bet you know who he works for."

"Indeed, now I do. Alyssa Ross. So, what was *her* role back when the bagman was recruited by her fixer? That pitch to me about a personal favor is looking very transparent. She apparently had a significant role in the kickback scheme... maybe it was even *her* plan to begin with and not her son-in-law's. Getting me to back off was self-preservation and not a mother's concern for her daughter. One more piece of the puzzle fits in place.

"The bank VP allowed me, for no extra charge, to briefly look over the record of money transfers into the account. Several transfers took place in the weeks *after* Lester had disappeared. Why would Eric Dillon continue making payments if his payee was gone? Because *he* didn't *know* Lester had disappeared. Because *he* wasn't responsible for that deed. Alyssa and company had made Lester disappear and neglected to tell Eric right away. That makes the most sense."

"Leslie, the story comes together but it only means that Alyssa has an even greater reason to stop it from seeing daylight."

"You're right, Ivy. Y'know, sometimes you work a story and you're in danger but don't know it. So, you plunge ahead. In this case the danger is apparent and makes you think twice if the price of the story is worth it. It's easy to say that comes with the job and a good reporter isn't deterred by danger. That's only true in crime fiction, not in real life."

"I'm not sure how to advise you, Les. I don't want to lose a friend over a story."

Leslie sat in an easy chair and contemplated her new storyline. Another bulb lit up in her brain. *It's possible that Alyssa is the behind-the-scenes head of AllCare and her son-in-law only the nominal CEO. The major moves are plotted by the mother-in-law. It was in her self-interest.*

AllCare profits are considerable, and Alyssa doesn't seem like the kind of person to let that situation out of her grasp. I wouldn't be surprised if she had other benefits from being involved with AllCare. She's clever and ruthless. Her son-in-law is on a long leash and makes most business moves on his own, like fouling up the hip joint purchase for a very tidy profit. That fiasco is going to land squarely on his shoulders.

At least now the fog had lifted, and the enemy was in clear sight.

CHAPTER 84

John Livingstone sat with his fingers forming his favorite chapel formation. His chin rested on the peak of the chapel's roof. He listened straight-faced as Leslie explained her new understanding of AllCare and the role of Alyssa Ross in managing it.

"Quite a detective you turned out to be, Ms. Nugent. The story is a mixture of good evidence and some pivotal conjecture. Don't know how far we can push the conjecture. I like the part about the bagman, the sketch artist, and Ivy recognizing the guy she met in place of you. You run with it from there, quite imaginatively. It feels right, but *is it* right?"

"My concern is a selfish one, John. I'm stepping on someone's big toe and that person doesn't want me to threaten her. She'll want her son-in-law to take the heat for the kickbacks and probably buy him some soft punishment. She's used to being in control and won't like some meddlesome reporter pointing an accusatory finger at her.

"She can probably have her way with the authorities once her son-in-law is convinced to take the fall. His confession undermines my story that has her at the helm. Maybe that gets her off my back. My story will use her fairy tale in place of the more truthful yarn I'd like to print."

"Exactly, Leslie. She can control the facts you have to report. *C'est la guerre.*"

"I think I'll visit Eric Dillon again and see if he's ready to take the dive. If so, Alyssa Ross wins this round. I might come back later with the real story."

CHAPTER 85

The AllCare office in White Plains was exactly as she remembered it from her visit several months earlier. The same secretary guarded the door to Dillon's office. The magazines and newspapers on the coffee table were up-to-date. Leslie was unsure how to approach Dillon. Based on their prior meeting she knew he could be evasive. Nevertheless, she needed to have him confirm or deny parts of her new understanding about payments to Lester Brandt.

She was ushered into the president's office and found a much-subdued Eric Dillon standing alongside his desk.

"Round two, Ms. Nugent? Seems our previous meeting ended in a draw; you didn't come away with any new information."

"That was then, Mr. Dillon. This is now. I'm much better prepared. Ready for a few questions?"

"Depends how invasive they are. Try me."

"Were you responsible for the payments to Lester Brandt?"

"Try another one, Miss Nugent. I'm gonna pass on that one."

"Put another way, are you prepared to accept responsibility for the payments even if you were only a passive player?"

"Again, I'm going to have to take a pass."

"Okay, let's cut to the chase. I know the bagman recruited to do the money transfers was hired out of your mother-in-law's office. Her fixer did the hiring. You only managed the payments. I know you continued payments to Lester Brandt's

Cayman account *after* he disappeared, suggesting you didn't even know he was gone. And I mean *gone*.

"Your mother-in-law is desperate to keep me from filling out the story behind the kickbacks because she, not you, controls AllCare. She set you up to take any blame for AllCare's unwise business decisions and now you're set to be the fall guy for the kickback scheme with Lester Brandt. She'll buy you a light sentence, probably just a fine. How am I doing so far, Mr. Dillon?"

"You're not going to get me to corroborate any of your wild accusations. I'll only offer you this: a warning. You're swimming in dangerous water and it's way over your head. Get back on dry land and write whatever you think you can substantiate. You might still be safe if you settle for that."

Leslie walked to the door and Eric Dillon followed quietly. She turned as she passed out of the office.

"I think I can take care of myself, Mr. Dillon. Can you say the same about yourself?"

She headed across the hall to the elevators and disappeared when the doors closed behind her.

The information she obtained from the Cayman bank made a more compelling case for her DA friend, Pat, than the lean presentation she'd made weeks before in the same office. Leslie's suspicions about Alyssa Ross were not included in the updated information. That would come out if a full-scale investigation was launched.

"I'll take the case to my boss," said the assistant DA, "and see if he thinks we have enough to open an investigation. You've done a helluva detective job, Leslie. I assume you're planning a follow-up story to your initial piece about the hips. Just be careful not to overextend yourself where the information is incomplete or nonexistent."

"Thanks. Pat. Let me know the decision as soon as you have one."

CHAPTER 86

The bleeding was not being controlled. This was Gene Lindell's eighth hip redo and it was proving to be his most difficult. Edith Varilla's procedure should have been like the three previous ones; through an anterior approach, remove the defective hip prosthesis, and replace it with a new Collier device. The procedure should have taken less than three hours. Here he was four hours later still trying to staunch the bleeding.

It brought to mind a similar scene when he was a medical student on his OB/GYN rotation. He could visualize a very seasoned surgeon, sitting on a stool, peering into a patient's perineum. A nurse was mopping the sweat off his brow as he struggled to achieve hemostasis an hour after the simple procedure should have ended.

Now here he was, repeating that scene. The only difference was the procedure, a hip replacement instead of a hysterectomy.

The initial incision and exposure had been routine until he saw a very poorly defined operative field. Healing had been disrupted by the hip joint's instability, leading to the body's disorganized effort to stabilize the joint with scar tissue. The blood supply to the hip joint area was similarly disorganized. Despite a very careful dissection, bleeding had been difficult to control. Two units of blood set up before surgery had already been given and two more were on order.

The blood bank called to say that the patient's blood type

made it difficult to type and match the units. There would be a delay of thirty minutes or more before the blood would be sent.

The patient's blood pressure was low, and the anesthesiologist had increased the rate of fluid administration. He now added a pressor agent to support her pressure. The blood was needed *now*. The patient was slipping into shock.

Lindell was beside himself. They could lose the patient on a simple hip joint replacement operation. When the blood arrived, the patient had already been hypotensive for nearly half an hour. He finally was able to stop the bleeding and send the patient to the recovery room. It appeared that they might have salvaged the situation until the patient showed no signs of awakening from the anesthesia. Lindell's worst fear was being realized: the eighty-two-year-old woman had not withstood the prolonged period of low blood pressure. Brain damage was the likely consequence. An EEG confirmed that grim diagnosis.

The patient was scheduled for transfer out of recovery with an IV running and a bladder catheter in place. Aside from the potential brain deficit, she was stable.

Her only child, a son, Anthony Varilla, was given the sad news by Lindell. The patient had been a widow for three years and had no other children. Varilla was distraught and had to be lightly sedated in a room off the waiting area.

He'd been hostile about the need for repeat surgery only three years after the initial replacement. After reading the article in *the Times* about the scandal involving AllCare in the hip joint fiasco he focused his anger on that company and its president, Eric Dillon.

CHAPTER 86

Leslie's friend in the DA's office called to give her the news: her boss, the Manhattan district attorney, didn't think they had enough of a case to go forward. He appreciated her effort and was going to keep the matter in his pending file in case any more evidence turned up that might change his mind. Leslie was disappointed but wasn't going to let it die. She didn't know what her next move would be, but she'd continue to cogitate.

After her meeting with Eric Dillon, she'd hoped the message he'd convey back to his mother-in-law would satisfy her that she was in no danger from the reporter. Recalling Dillon's advice that she stick to information she could corroborate, she believed Alyssa would realize that the reporter didn't have enough hard evidence to represent a threat to her personally.

CHAPTER 88

Letitia Dillon's bunion/hammertoe surgery was healing nicely according to the orthopedic resident on evening rounds; he told her she was cleared to go home tomorrow. Her husband, Eric Dillon, dutifully delivered the clothes she wanted for the trip home.

Two doors down, Gene Lindell was consoling Anthony Varilla as he delivered the test results confirming that his mother was severely brain damaged and would not recover any useful function. Anthony was disconsolate and seething with anger over the hand his mother had been dealt.

"It's not fair. It's just not fair. That bastard who sold the hospital those defective hips should be lying here in my mother's place. We did what we were told to do, and this is how it turns out. I don't blame you, Dr. Lindell. You did your best."

The doctor consoled the grieving son and made his exit. A nurse came in and asked Anthony to step outside while she and an aide changed the bedsheets.

In the hallway Anthony wandered aimlessly down the row of rooms. As he passed Letitia Dillon's room a nurse was coming out. She paused in the doorway.

"I'll send an aide with a wheelchair to help you and Letitia to your car, Mr. Dillon." The nurse left.

Varilla stopped. The door to the room was open. He recognized Eric Dillon from his picture in *the Times* article detailing the whole hip joint tragedy. Anthony carried the article with him as a morbid reminder of how he and his mother had gotten into this situation.

Dillon saw the stranger looking into the room and went to close the door. Anthony saw him coming and yelled at him, "You murdered my mother, you bastard!"

Dillon stopped with one hand on the door. The look on his face was one of total surprise. Anthony rushed at him, and they tumbled to the floor. Dillon's head hit the tile floor hard, stunning him. The enraged attacker began to punch the semiconscious man and bang his head against the floor. When Anthony realized his victim was unconscious, he got off him and fled the room.

Security arrived and nurses tended to the victim. Hysterical, Letitia Dillon wouldn't stop screaming. Nurses told the security police who the attacker was and that he had gone into the stairwell.

Anthony Varilla was stopped and arrested in the parking lot. Eric Dillon was rushed to the emergency room and found to have a fractured skull with massive brain damage. He was pronounced dead in the ER.

CHAPTER 89

Despite the pall hanging over the Ross-Taylor household, Alyssa knew that the death of Eric Dillon had been a blessing in disguise for her. Any investigation of kickbacks and bribery involving AllCare would come to a halt when it got to Eric's involvement in the matter. He was the presumed guilty party and that would end the matter. There wouldn't be any incentive for the DA to pursue the case further. Her daughter's grief was something else.

Leslie was still stewing over the DA's disinclination to pursue the case she'd presented before Dillon's death. It just didn't sit well with her.

She and Ivy were having dinner with Diana Gold. Leslie brought Diana up to speed on the matter. They discussed the alternative; that Leslie just move on and give Alyssa a free pass she didn't deserve.

"I can't see how two people can see the evidence so differently, Ivy. Dawson Nichols is a very respected attorney, a former prosecutor, and a tough-on-crime DA."

Diana offered a new insight. "Well, what are we missing, Leslie? What about this case is turning him off? Maybe it's not the evidence but something else about the case that's contrary to his self-interest."

"You may be onto something, Di. The DA is an elected official just like the governor. How would this case be an adverse factor in his reelection bid? I sure would like to see a list of his major donors in the last election. Can I use your computer?"

"Be my guest Leslie. I'm betting on what you're going to

find out. I'm writing down my prediction on this piece of paper."

Diana pulled her laptop from her carryall bag, cleared space on the table in front of Leslie, and opened the computer. Leslie brought up Google. She typed in "Dawson Nichols large election donors." Google seemed to be waiting for this opportunity to strut its stuff. A list of major individual and nonindividual donors appeared in an instant. Alyssa Ross was one of the very generous individual donors and Ross-Wagner was a very generous nonindividual donor. If you added her husband's donation, the couple was the largest individual donor to Dawson Nichols's most recent election campaign.

"Okay. Seems like we're onto something. What was your prediction, Diana?"

"Read it yourself." She handed the slip of paper to Leslie and sat back in an easy chair grinning like a Cheshire cat.

"You had it figured, lawyer-lady. Good show. Now, how to use this information. It's not a secret. All you need is a computer and the know-how to do a Google search. I bet Alyssa Ross is pretty smug now that her son-in-law is out of the way. The kickbacks will be pinned on him and he's not here to defend himself. I think my story has just added a new dimension: large donor insurance. Trouble is I lack confirmation for my strong suspicion. My crucial witnesses are either gone or unlikely to turn on their boss. I think Alyssa is home safe and knows that I pose no threat to her. The DA has made me secure. Damn it."

Diana opined, "I agree, Leslie. Sometimes an orderly retreat is the best you can do. There are lots of other stories out there that don't place you in jeopardy. Just fold up your tent and move on. There's a good man in your life so make him your priority."

CHAPTER 90

Alyssa took Leslie's call and agreed to meet her at the Met. No agenda was specified but they both knew what was on the table. They found a quiet place to sit in the mostly empty restaurant and ordered a pot of tea.

Leslie was quick to steer the conversation into the contentious area.

"Alyssa, I want to call a truce. I know a lot about your role in the AllCare debacle. I don't question your concern about your daughter's reputation in the face of an AllCare kickback scandal, but that was just a smokescreen to shield *your* role in the kickback activity. You've been a bad girl but are clever enough to stay out of sight. Lucky, too. Eric's death plays right into your hand."

Alyssa cut in. "Let's jump ahead, Leslie. I know what cards you're holding. All of them. I know the case you tried to get the DA to take on. You failed. If it's a truce you want, okay. I want this mess to be over. I don't have anything to fear from you so let's declare a truce, shake hands and move on."

"Okay, Alyssa. I figured the DA would get back to you. I saw your donor record for his campaigns. He owes you, big. That's another facet to this story that I'm going to sit on. Let me be clear. The story you want me to throw away is sitting in my attorney's hands with instructions to bring it back to life if anything untoward happens to me. He'll turn it over to my editor and I assure you that will bring it back to life."

"I admire your tenacity, Leslie. Knowing when to fish and when to cut bait is another enviable trait."

Alyssa offered her hand for a handshake agreement but Leslie was not inclined to take it. They parted with a smile instead. Leslie reflected, a *truce* is not necessarily the *end* of a conflict, only a cessation of hostilities of uncertain duration.

There'd be another DA eventually, she thought, maybe one interested in what she had to offer. One of Alyssa's inner circle might become disenchanted with their participation in some very unsavory schemes. New information about the kickbacks might surface in the papers of Lester Brandt or Eric Dillon. The large cover-up could unravel if a loose thread was left hanging.

Sure, this was wishful thinking, but that's what she was left with at the moment.

Walking down the stairs out of the Met, Leslie smiled to herself. She had unburdened herself of a story that seemingly had no end and kept her tied up in knots. Maybe for the first time she had her priorities straight. Brad was important; he was number one in her life. No story would be allowed to take her eyes off that prize. With that realization, her future seemed brighter than it had looked when she walked up the stairs into the museum.

CHAPTER 91

THREE MONTHS LATER

Leslie and Brad were drinking their morning coffee in the kitchen of his apartment. Leslie's phone rang. She recognized the caller: Pat Coleman, in the DA's office.

"Hey, Pat. This is an unexpected call at nine in the morning."

"Hope I didn't wake you."

"No, no. Tell me why you called. Must be something important since we haven't spoken for months."

"Well, you'll be interested in what I have to offer up. It's a follow-up to the story you told me several months ago in my office. Listen up. A snitch we have in Attica reported that a con he knows was boasting about a guy he made disappear. This con is in for life based on a conviction for armed robbery during which a guard was killed. Shortly before his robbery fiasco he was hired by a guy he never saw before, based on his reputation for doing away with victims and leaving no evidence behind. He was given twenty-five grand up front to make some white-collar dude disappear. A second twenty-five was to be paid when the job was done. He did the deed and was paid by a drop. He never saw the payor a second time."

"Okay. Why are you calling *me*?"

"Out of the goodness of my heart, I remembered the story you told me and the fact that the kickback recipient had disappeared. Could be this gone-guy or maybe not. I'm going up to Attica to meet the magician and find out if he's for real and wants to do some trading. He's not getting out of his life sentence but there may be some perks we can offer in exchange for a body."

"And how do I figure in?"

"I'll take you along to see if his story has any credibility. It's more than unusual that I do this but I'm willing to stick my neck out a little bit. Interested?"

"Tell me when and where we'll meet."

"I thought you'd bite. I wanted some company on the long drive and I thought of you. I'll pick you up tomorrow morning at eight. It's a five- to six-hour ride so you can snooze in the car. We'll have a driver take us in a city car. The con already agreed to meet and says he'll have a lawyer with him."

CHAPTER 92

Leslie fell asleep an hour out of New York City and woke up an hour from Attica. The prison was an impressive, formidable, concrete fortress. Not inviting in any way. Patricia and Leslie were escorted into a windowless room where they were searched and told the rules for visitors. Their phones were taken away and their handbags put in canvas bags for safekeeping. Next, they were escorted to a barren room with a table and four chairs, three on one side and one on the other side of a plastic divider.

Pat and Leslie introduced themselves to Philip Corrente, the convict's attorney. Corrente indicated that he had flown up from LaGuardia Airport that afternoon. The three took chairs and, as soon as they were settled, the door to the room opened and a prisoner in an orange jumpsuit and ankle bracelets was ushered in by a guard who quickly left.

The prisoner sat down opposite the three visitors, separated by the plastic divider. Corrente introduced his client as Arthur Snead.

"I won't bother with detailing Arthur's status. You two have had ample time to read the email I sent you describing his situation. Arthur has information that may prove of interest to you. In exchange for the information, he's asking that certain 'perks' be extended to him. He has no illusion that his sentence will be reduced. Similarly, he asks that no additional penalty be imposed if facts come out that incriminate him. Since his sentence is life without opportunity for parole it's difficult to envision any other sentence being laid on him. Shall we proceed?"

The two women nodded in the affirmative.

"Arthur, I'm Patricia Coleman, an assistant district attorney in New York City and this is Leslie Nugent, a reporter with *The New York Times*. Why don't you begin your story?"

Arthur Snead had been in Attica a little over six months and showed no signs of physical deterioration. A lean, well-muscled man, he looked no more than his fifty years. He was clean-shaven with a receding hairline. A friendly smile revealed teeth in reasonable repair. In short, there was nothing at first glance to indicate this man was sociopathic and homicidal.

"About a year ago I received a call on my cell phone from a person I did not know. He asked that we meet to discuss a proposition I would find attractive. He was very vague. We met at a place of his choosing. He handed me a sealed envelope with a single sheet of paper containing some facts about an intended victim along with a photograph. This delivery man claimed to be 'uninformed,' his exact word, about the proposition spelled out in the envelope. The terms of payment were spelled out on the paper. I would be paid twenty-five Gs up front and twenty-five more when the job was completed. That was it. I told him I would accept the assignment. He handed me another envelope with twenty-five thousand dollars in it and left. I did the job and was paid the additional twenty-five at a designated drop. I only saw him that one time."

"Do you recall the name of the vic? I presume the victim was a man?"

"I do. He was Lester Brandt, an exec at Metro Hospital in Manhattan."

Leslie's jaw dropped but no sound came out of her open mouth.

Snead proceeded to tell how he made Brandt disappear.

Pat spoke dryly. "We need to retrieve the body to confirm the victim's identity. Can you help us do that?"

"Don't see why not. But first let's talk about perks. I have a list of special conditions which can make my life easier in a caged environment. Number one would be transfer to a more friendly facility. You can read the rest. None of them are a big stretch so I think, in the interest of fairness, you should make an effort to carry out your part of the bargain. If you do, you'll have the body."

"That's fair Mr. Snead. We'll see how far we can go. Leslie, do you have any questions for Arthur?"

"Just a few, Pat. Arthur, could you recognize the man who hired you?"

"Possibly. He wasn't disguised but he stayed in the shadows. We were only together for a few minutes. Show me a picture and I'll give it a shot."

"Fair enough," was Leslie's response. "One last question. Did you get his name?"

Snead shook his head in firm denial.

Leslie smiled. "I didn't think so. That would have made our job too easy."

Corrente stood up and indicated the session was over. "Pat, get back to me with your response to Arthur's wish list. Then we can talk 'body.'"

On the drive back to New York City, Pat studied the con's wish list; there was room to give. Leslie told Pat about the artist's drawing of the man who hired the bagman who made the deposits to Brandt's offshore account. They agreed to use the drawing in a photo array if they could get the same police artist to produce five other similar drawings of men. That would be the lineup they would present to Snead, asking him to identify the man who handed him the sealed envelope containing the offer to disappear Lester Brandt.

The two were encouraged by the visit.

The police artist had files of drawings made over the years listening to witnesses describe people for him to draw from their memories. Leslie and Pat, along with the artist, sifted through a large pile of drawings. They came up with five older ones that were similar in technique, size, and expression. They all three agreed on one drawing of their unknown guy that fit comfortably in the photo array format of six men. It was a very fair lineup for identification purposes.

CHAPTER 93

This time they flew up to Attica. Pat had agreed with all of Snead's requests with the exception of "female visitations"; *that* she assumed was thrown in as a joke.

They met with Snead and his lawyer in the same room they'd interviewed him in. First, Pat told Snead that his wish list had been approved by the prosecutor who'd sent him to Attica. She didn't tell him how much wrangling they'd done to get agreement. They handed his lawyer a copy of their agreed upon perks. Second, Pat explained the picture array and laid it on the table in front of Snead. She simply asked him if he could identify the man who hired him.

"Piece-a-cake," he said, after a brief perusal of the array. "It's number three." Snead pointed to the drawing of the man who hired the bagman.

Pat cautioned him, "It's important that you be sure. Take more time if you need to. We're in no hurry."

Snead studied the array again. "I'm sure. It's a good likeness."

Pat turned to Corrente. "We're satisfied that we conducted a fair lineup. Do you agree, Mr. Corrente?"

The attorney nodded in agreement. "I believe the process was conducted without prejudice or undue pressure. My client cooperated fully."

Pat took back the array.

"Now Mr. Snead, can we talk 'body'?"

"Yeah, I'm satisfied. I want to get out of this hellhole. The body's buried in the woods in a state park in Westchester County. I'll have to take you there. I can't give you directions to the site."

Pat nodded her head in the affirmative. "I'll arrange for the trip, Mr. Snead. If all goes well and the body is identified as Lester Brandt, you'll be on your way to better lodgings."

Pat looked over to Leslie who'd stayed silent during the proceedings.

"Ms. Nugent. Any questions or thoughts?"

Leslie stood up and looked at Snead. "Thanks for your cooperation. The identification process today will help move a major case along that defied closure. I have nothing else to say, Ms. Coleman."

The foursome adjourned.

On the way to the airport Leslie and Pat agreed the witness was crucial.

"Assuming we find Lester Brandt's body, we clear up a missing person case, have a murder to prosecute with the confessed murderer in custody, and the start of a trail back to his probable employer. Not a bad catch. Trouble is we don't know the name of the man the witnesses identified. We also hope an ID from an artist's sketch will hold up in court. Keep your fingers crossed, Leslie."

"I'm looking ahead to the trail we've uncovered. We got a lot of mileage out of an artist's drawing."

CHAPTER 94

The body was well-concealed but Snead had no difficulty leading the police through the woods to the burial site. The medical examiner identified the body as Lester Brandt based on dental records and DNA. Pat called Leslie with the news. The trips to Attica had paid off handsomely.

So, *who* was the person who hired a man to make kickback money transfers to Lester Brandt and "innocently" recruited the hitman to murder Lester Brandt? Most important, he was also identified by Ivy from the same artist drawing used in the picture array presented to Arthur Snead.

Based on Ivy's experience with the unidentified man, Leslie had surmised a connection with Alyssa Ross. Early that morning she cabbed over to the Ross-Wagner office building and showed the drawing to the security desk person. This yielded a name to go with the picture: Luke Rollins. His role in Lester Brandt's murder plot still hinged on the reliability of testimony and identification by Arthur Snead, a convicted felon.

Walking out of the Ross-Wagner building Leslie had to marvel at her good fortune. All that digging had paid off big-time. She wanted to pat herself on the back but she knew that Arthur Snead had just fallen into her lap, and Ivy's serendipitous ID of the face in the drawing was not due to hard work. Now, walking slowly up Fifth Avenue, she considered her next step in the story, spurred on by this giant step forward.

An interview with Luke Rollins before she turned in his name to Pat would greatly enrich her story. Once he was arrested and lawyered up it would be too late. The pressure of time was filling her sails and propelling her to act without delay. She had a sense that her current advantage could dissolve as quickly as it had evolved. She hopped into a cab and headed to her preferred car rental agency.

For a fifty dollar bill the same security man had been only too happy to provide an address for Luke Rollins, so Leslie drove up the Saw Mill River Parkway to Dobbs Ferry early that afternoon. On the way she called his office and learned that he hadn't been seen all day.

Rollins lived in an unpretentious private house. The house was dark. The garage was empty. The mailbox was full. This morning's *New York Times* lay in the driveway. Indications were that he had left the house early this morning or yesterday evening. She parked her car down the street where she had a good view of the house. Her plan was to give him plenty of time to appear before assuming he wasn't going to show.

Hours later she became convinced her stakeout was making a point. Luke Rollins was not to be found. A final call to his office confirmed that he'd been a no-show all day and his secretary had no idea where he was. Leslie was able to squeeze a little bio information from his secretary; Luke was divorced and lived alone. His cell phone number was passed along and calls went unanswered except by voicemail.

Leslie considered three possibilities. One: he was away on business or pleasure. She considered this unlikely since his secretary would have known. Two: he had fled in fear that Alyssa Ross would silence him before he was arrested. Three: he had already been silenced.

She doubted his body was in the house since there was

no car in the garage. The front door was locked and no one answered the doorbell. She had called from the car driving up and there was no answer other than an invitation to leave a voicemail. Leslie was uneasy.

Sitting in her car, she went over the facts relating to Rollins's newly discovered identification. Aside from any accomplice(s) in the AllCare matter, she, Leslie Nugent, was the only one who knew of Rollins's involvement. The ADA knew the face, *but not his name.* Only Leslie had the gift ID from Ivy that eventually affixed his name to the drawing and tied him to Alyssa Ross.

But wait, she thought, *why would Rollins feel endangered?* Even *he* didn't know that he'd been identified by Leslie. Or did he? It was just hours ago that Leslie had been given his name by the security person at the Ross-Wagner building. Had that employee tipped off Luke?

Ouch, she thought. Her friend Pat had probably updated her boss, Dawson Nichols, on what she knew. The ID, albeit without a name, brought AllCare front and center along with the payola scheme he'd brushed away previously. He was uncomfortably close to Alyssa Ross, his prime campaign supporter. If she heard about the sketch ID from Nichols, as a party with an interest in AllCare, she'd know that Leslie was dangerously close and that Luke would soon be in the hands of the authorities.

Even if Nichols didn't pass on any information to Alyssa, the security guard at Ross's building, thinking about his Christmas bonus, might have reported back to her that a woman was seeking to ID Luke Rollins from a sketch.

Leslie thus imagined several ways Alyssa Ross could know that her close associate was a target of the persistent reporter. She'd want him silenced, quickly. The security guard most likely called Rollins first, at home that morning, letting him know that a newspaper reporter was interested in his identity. In that case he might have chosen to make himself scarce.

Too many leaks were possible, she thought.

CHAPTER 95

From previous updates by Assistant DA Pat Coleman, Dawson Nichols knew a payola scheme might have been operating between AllCare and Metro, but the disappearance of Brandt and the death of Dillon had made prosecution unappealing. Who would he prosecute? Now, new evidence, albeit unusual, about a common hirer of the bagman and Brandt's killer brought the payola issue back to life. Alyssa Ross's deceased son-in-law was entwined in these issues. He'd have Pat Coleman meet with Alyssa to learn what light she might shed on her son-in-law's character and his relationship with Lester Brandt.

He'd given this AllCare-Metro story a pass in recent months but didn't want to get caught asleep at the switch as it developed further in his own backyard. He valued Alyssa's financial support and didn't think she'd take offense at this benign inquiry.

Late that afternoon Pat Coleman arrived in an unmarked city car at the Ross-Wagner building. Alyssa greeted her at the door to her office. She'd sent her staff home early.

"Greetings, Ms. Coleman. Come in and relax." They shook hands.

Alyssa ushered her into her office and guided her to a comfortable easy chair. She took the opposite chair and spread her arms.

"Okay. I know this isn't a social call, so tell me why we're meeting. I've been trying to imagine any possible reason you'd be knocking at my door."

"Okay, Ms. Ross. I'll dive right in. I'm a good friend of a reporter from *the Times*. The reporter has laid out a case that AllCare and Metro were involved in a payola scheme giving AllCare a virtual monopoly at Metro. The purchasing VP at Metro was the pivotal figure. His disappearance and the tragic death of your son-in-law rendered any action on my office's part moot since those were the two suspected players in the payola scheme.

"So, the matter lay dormant. Now the reporter has uncovered a bagman who was hired to make the payola payments to the Metro VP. Then serendipity struck and the VP's murderer came forward. The bagman and the murderer have identified the same man as the one who hired them. Admittedly, his precise identity has not yet been established."

"That's quite a story, Ms. Coleman. So where do I fit in? Why are you telling me this tale? I'm more than a little curious."

"The reporter told me that you had asked her to back off the story for personal reasons. Now the story has moved forward with the same unidentified person hiring the bagman and a murderer. Your son-in-law's death hasn't eliminated him as a possible suspect behind this mess. My boss is ready to let the matter go back to the dead case file but he'd like to know if you have any insight into this tale that might extend its life and prove an embarrassment to the DA."

Alyssa put on her most earnest deadpan. "I appreciate you giving me an opportunity to clear the air where *my* involvement is concerned. My personal issue, the one I asked the reporter to respect, was the potential scandal Eric, my son-in-law, could be involved in. That would hurt my daughter. I wanted the reporter to let it go before it went public. With

Eric's death and the unlikelihood of a big case coming forward, my mother's anxiety was quelled. I fear Eric might have been behind the bagman recruitment and possibly the VP's murder. I suspect he may have wanted the VP eliminated to defuse the whole AllCare-Metro matter. That's just my conjecture. I don't know it for a fact."

"One last question. Did you think your son-in-law was capable of planning a murder? This gets to the question of character. I know that's a reach but it's a question the DA wanted me to ask."

"I'm no expert on judging character, Ms. Coleman, so my answer is rather general; I think anyone is capable of murder given the right set of circumstances. Eric was under a lot of pressure and may have felt his partner in the payola scheme was becoming unreliable. In that context, I think he may have considered extreme measures. Who knows?"

Coleman sat forward and stared to the floor.

"Okay, Ms. Ross. I had to ask. My boss's neck is stuck out a bit further than he finds comfortable. I guess we'll have to ease off until I can identify the mystery man in the sketch."

"That sounds like a good ending to a curious story. I hope you can get your reporter friend to follow the same advice."

They both stood as if on command and headed out to the elevator.

As soon as the door closed, Alyssa began muttering to herself. Luke would have to be taken care of. Fortunately, even if he was identified as the mystery man who did the hiring, Alyssa had left no fingerprints to connect *her* to the actions he'd taken. The blame would still lay with the now deceased Eric Dillon. He was the one who used the bagman and saw Lester Brandt as a very shaky partner in the payola operation. Luke Rollins was acting at Dillon's behest.

The security guard in the building was a loyal soldier but

had initially failed to warn her about the snooping reporter. She called down to the desk and learned that Luke had been tipped off first, not her. If the reporter got to him and he opened up, Alyssa's involvement in these matters could prove embarrassing to say the least. Luke would see that, once identified as the hirer, he represented a serious threat to Alyssa. She also realized he might be hard to find.

She had danced around the matter of the reporter's tenacious pursuit long enough. Too long, she thought. She was dangerous and relentless. She had to go. Alyssa's business strategy was passed down from her father: don't hesitate to eliminate threats, even if those threats are embodied in associates close to you. She held steadfast to that strategy.

CHAPTER 96

With a late winter weekend looming and Doug in Florida getting in shape for the season opener in three weeks, Ivy asked Leslie and Brad to spend the weekend with her in her "Country House" as she called it. Leslie liked the idea and volunteered to bring enough food so they wouldn't have to leave the house until it was time to return to the Big Apple. One hitch: Brad would have to drive up alone later that evening since he had a consequential late afternoon conference on Friday.

Ivy picked up Leslie at her apartment building as the winter sun was beginning to set. The two women were soon on their way north, but were not alone. Tailing them in a Subaru minivan were two men with a simple mission: terminate the reporter and, if necessary, anyone with her. Leslie matched the woman in the photo they were given as well as the printed description. The woman accompanying her was of no interest to them.

The drive took about an hour and a half in Friday late afternoon traffic. When they were just a few miles from the house, Ivy shared a suspicion with Leslie.

"I think we picked up a tail somewhere along the way. Up here it would be hard for a tail to stay invisible; the car traffic is so light. I saw this minivan following us for the last ten minutes or so. I don't think they're fans of mine, Leslie. What do you think?"

Ivy stole a glance at her friend.

"From the look on your face, Leslie, it's obvious who they might be looking for. And it's not me."

Leslie had little doubt that Alyssa Ross was aware of her progress in unraveling the AllCare mystery. Alyssa surely knew Leslie was a threat to turn in Luke. His disappearance made sense, whether he was hiding out or sanctioned by Alyssa. The pieces in the puzzle fit very neatly. The one remaining piece wasn't hard to figure. Leslie could feel Alyssa ready to fit her in the last remaining opening.

"Leslie, I think we need to quickly get in the house and prepare a welcome for our uninvited guests."

When they arrived at the house, they drove up the long driveway and into the garage. There'd only been traces of snow along the roadside, a sign of the mild winter they'd experienced.

The house hadn't been used for several weeks so it would take a while to warm up. Ivy quickly started a fire in the woodstove. She'd left it set up for this when she and Doug last stayed over. Leslie quickly carried in the bags of food. She refrigerated what had to stay cold and left the rest on a kitchen counter. The two next carried in their weekend travel bags and dropped them in the hallway leading to the two first-floor bedrooms.

The two women stood in front of the warming woodstove in the large living area. Ivy cooly took charge of their team.

"Listen closely, Leslie. When we turned into the drive our tail continued past; it didn't have much choice. In the master bedroom on this floor are two handguns. Doug and I felt secure here knowing we were armed, considering the relative isolation of the house. I'm going to get them."

Ivy quickly headed for the bedroom and returned with two menacing guns: Sig Sauer P320 Compact 9mms. She handed one to Leslie and indicated the safety catch.

Leslie had noted a distinct change in Ivy's tone and behavior since they arrived at the house. She was pumped up and comfortably in control as she contemplated the danger they faced.

Leslie on the other hand was trembling in anticipation of the coming confrontation. She sensed that Ivy's alternative personality had kicked in to deal with the threatening situation.

"Doug did a little research and came up with this nine millimeter which has a fifteen-round magazine. Les, can you shoot?"

"I'm not an expert marksman but I've been to ranges and even took a few classes in self-defense. Sometimes I'm chasing a story and it takes me into places I'd rather not go into unarmed. How about you?"

"Same as you, Leslie. Some training using this gun. I'm not a bad marksman but I've never shot with anyone shooting at *me*. Okay, I suggest we take up positions where we can't be seen through any windows. I'll get behind that stuffed chair and you duck behind the large sofa. The doors are locked so if these guys want *in*, they'll either pick a lock or just burst in. I don't think we'll see their car. They'll park where we can't see it and walk to the house."

"Ivy, assuming they followed us from the city, they know they were tailing two *women*. They might be a bit overconfident, drive up to the house, and try the simplest approach: knocking on the door."

"Not bad reasoning. As a matter of fact, a car's headlights just came up the driveway and I see two unfamiliar guys getting out. They're heading to our front door. Let's keep out of sight and let them make the first move. Safety catch off, Leslie. If they break in we're ready to shoot. Let's let them separate and start searching for us."

A loud knocking on the door added to the already high level of tension. The women remained silent and well-concealed. The chair and sofa were far apart and flanked the woodstove. Leslie could feel the perspiration under her arms. Ivy was cool and determined.

A second knocking went unanswered.

"Hello in there. Anyone home? We had some car trouble and need to use your phone. We can't get any cell service out here."

The men outside were frustrated. Their simple approach had failed. They needed a more aggressive strategy. For all they knew the women inside had just called the police. There was no time to waste.

A very hard boot struck the front door. It splintered somewhat and gave way. The two men entered the dimly lit, spacious living room cautiously with guns drawn, but saw no human targets. They separated and started to search the house; one headed down the hallway to the left leading to the bedrooms and the other started straight back toward the kitchen.

Ivy peered around her stuffed chair and saw an opportunity. She rose quickly and fired a burst of three quick shots at the latter's back. She saw him fall but she quickly ducked back down in her hiding place. The man heading down the hallway to the bedrooms turned in time to see his partner fall. He moved cautiously back into the living area looking for the shooter. Leslie saw him moving away from her, in a crouch. She stood up as he passed and, with a shaking hand, fired two shots at his back. One missed and the other hit him in the lower back, just above the left buttock. The wounded gunman rose up, spun around and caught another shot, mid-chest, from Ivy.

The adrenalized women came forward cautiously to witness the carnage. Ivy's first man was dead. Leslie's man was lying on his back, coughing blood but conscious. Ivy's hit was the one likely to prove fatal.

Ivy called 911 and requested the police and an ambulance. Leslie had wet her pants but was surprised how calm she now felt considering the danger she'd just been exposed to. The entire action had lasted less than a minute but seemed a lot longer. She tried talking to the wounded man but he was unable or unwilling to speak.

The Mount Kisco police arrived, followed shortly by an ambulance with EMT personnel. The rescue team moved the wounded man to the ambulance and sped off to the hospital.

The police were stunned to find two gunmen taken out by two young women who came through unharmed. The details of their defensive moves were taken down by the lead officer who continually shook his head in amazement.

"You gals ever been in combat before?" the officer asked.

Ivy quipped, "Fought off a few gropers in my time but never used a gun. I think these guys were after more than a feel."

He laughed.

Leslie was amazed at her friend's composure. On reflection she ascribed it to Ivy's personality disorder. She was coming down from a high as her aggressive persona began to recede.

The police asked the women to come to police headquarters the next day to give formal statements. For tonight, they'd let them calm down after surviving the assault. The lead officer and one of his lieutenants still marveled at how well one of the women seemed to handle the life-threatening attack while her partner was still shaken by the encounter.

An officer was assigned to stay in the house overnight and come to headquarters with the women in the morning. One patrol car was left conspicuously in the driveway.

CHAPTER 97

As the police were pulling out of the driveway, an astonished Brad Grossman drove up and waited for the police cars to clear out. He rushed into the house, taking note of the splintered front door hanging loosely from its hinges.

Leslie rushed to him. They embraced with an intense hug. When they parted, Brad saw that she was uninjured but tearful. He acknowledged Ivy with a forced smile as she came forward to give him a warm embrace.

"Leslie, what happened here? Tell me, for god's sake."

Ivy spoke up. "Brad, let me step in here and give Leslie some more time to regain her composure. I'll fill you in on a most remarkable evening. But first, let's sit down here and try to relax."

Ivy proceeded to recount the tale of the past few hours while Leslie huddled next to Brad on the sofa.

An hour later the scene was beginning to approximate what they'd all been looking forward to on their drive out of New York City: a modest blaze in the fireplace, a glass of wine, and a plate of cheeses on a low table within easy reach.

For Leslie though, a stiff scotch was more in order to help settle her jangled nerves. She found it hard to believe the present scene after the way the evening had begun. *Just a brief timeout,* she thought, *while we cut down two gunmen.*

Brad reflected on the mayhem just past. "Those guys weren't after Ivy, Leslie. Someone really has it in for *you.* You've kept me in the loop as far as your never-ending story goes, so I assume that's where the hostility is coming from. Trouble is there's no shortage of guns for hire, so thwarting this attack only means another one may be planned." He paused, briefly, and looked hard at Leslie. "I'm just thinking out loud. We have to do *something* to discourage your adversary from using this route to solve her issue with you."

"I agree, Brad. You're right! I'm sure I was the target and Ivy would have been collateral damage if we hadn't warded off the attack. I'm a toxic friend. You're absolutely right; I need to find a way to discourage any future attack."

The three grew silent, staring at the fire but deep in thought. Brad offered a possible solution.

"We have to level the playing field, Leslie. Ross has to know that a future attack on *you* will be met with a comparable attack on *her. Personally.* Now how do we make that threat *credible*? During the Cold War, neither side could risk launching a nuclear first strike; the retaliation potential, or second strike, made it too costly. Once submarines could fire nuclear missiles it became impossible to wipe out retaliatory potential.

"I remember learning about this in college during a course on post-WWII Europe. The term that stuck with me was 'rational deterrence.' The *catchier* term was 'mutual assured destruction.'

"Leslie, I think that concept is sound; it kept the Soviet Union and the US armed to the teeth but unwilling to use their atomic weaponry against each other. Now, *you* need a credible retaliation team. You then have to convince your adversary that this team, once set in motion, cannot be recalled from its mission. Did you see the movie *Fail Safe*? If not, watch it."

"I'm trying to imagine how I recruit such a team, Brad. It's a good gig for an underworld outfit. I pay them a standby or retainer fee and hope they're never called into action. I'm getting to like the idea."

Ivy had a slight smile on her face. "It's a variation on the old protection racket. How do we find a taker who has credibility? Maybe your policeman friend, Chan Young, can help us out, Les."

"Interesting suggestion, Ivy. I'll sound him out. Hopefully I can convince him that I'm not *planning* a crime but rather hoping to *prevent* one. He might just go for it or at least take it seriously."

Brad toasted, "Here's to mutual assured destruction." They touched glasses. Brad added, "During the Cold War that strategy's acronym was MAD. I'm uncertain how it will be received in your foe's camp. It hinges on credibility."

A fully restored Leslie added, "Now, let's turn our attention to the food and drink we toted up here."

Press and TV coverage of the attack and successful defense focused on the two women standing their ground and overcoming the attackers. There was no information about a motive for the assault. The story went from front page to local news in two days and then was old news with little or no follow-up.

Chan Young was uneasy about taking part in a potential crime but he understood the deterrence value. He agreed, with cautious reluctance, to try out the idea, incognito, on a few candidates he knew in the underworld. Not surprisingly, there were takers. One gang leader told him that MAD was the strategy competing gangs lived by. They avoided costly conflicts.

The strategy was put in place. It was not a bluff. Ivy agreed to handle the standby fee. She considered herself a potential beneficiary, hoping her role as collateral damage never came to fruition.

CHAPTER 98

Three days later, back in New York City, Leslie made the call to Alyssa Ross and they agreed to meet at the fountain in Lincoln Center Plaza at ten the next morning. The telephone conversation was curt and noninformational aside from the time and place of their meeting.

The two women arrived on time, unaccompanied by any associates. They greeted one another with a cordial head nod. Leslie spoke first without any emotion in her voice.

"Alyssa, I'm going to say my piece and leave. I wanted to deliver it in person. Please, don't interrupt me." She paused a moment and then continued, "Your attempt to silence me obviously failed but it set in motion my strategy to prevent any future attempt on my life. I don't intend to constantly be on guard. I can't let you control my future and possibly terminate it. I've set up a system of mutually assured destruction, similar to what the US and the Soviet Union recognized during the Cold War. *Any* attempt on *my* life, reasonably attributed to you, will be followed by a comparable assault on *your* life. *I'm making this personal.*

"The necessary steps have been taken and I'm putting you on notice *today* that you're a target if you chose to make me one again. I advise against testing the system to find out if it's operative. I'm not bluffing. That's all I wanted to say."

Leslie turned with a grim look on her face, and briskly

walked away from the fountain area. She felt the message had been clearly delivered.

Alyssa was left standing alone, unsure what to make of Leslie's threat.

CHAPTER 99

ONE MONTH LATER

Sitting across from each other in a dimly lit neighborhood bar, Leslie and Ivy reflected on the way they'd managed to bring a dangerous situation under control. At least for the time being.

"I guess the MAD strategy worked, Ivy. I thought it would, but wasn't sure. I guess sometimes you need to go outside your usual boundary of caution and go for broke."

"But not too often, Les. Let's remember that. Your way is best, so stay with your cautious, thoughtful way of operating."

Leslie could tell Ivy was anxious.

"Something's on your mind, Ivy. Let it out."

"There is something I need to tell you, Les." She paused, trying to contain her emotions. "I owe you big for pushing me into therapy. I know I was difficult and resistant to the idea that I needed help. You were my rock. You stayed on my case and helped me find an appropriate therapist. For that I'll be eternally grateful. I think I've gained some insight into my problem that I never would have achieved without help. I don't know if I'll ever be cured but I do think I have more control over my reactions."

She paused again and gave Leslie a sheepish smile. She then reached over and gave her a long embrace.

"I just had to say this and make sure you know what a

pivotal role you played in my life. I know it sounds terribly dramatic, but what would you expect from an actress?"

"Ivy, I couldn't be happier for you. I know it wasn't easy to accept but you had the determination to go on. I'm glad for both of us."

Leslie raised her glass. "To the future."

Glasses clinked and they both smiled broadly.

Later that evening, alone in her apartment, Leslie reflected on her friend's entry into therapy and Ivy's good fortune since they met. Her career had taken off, she'd ended an unhappy marriage, her financial future was secure, she was living with a super guy who was also a baseball legend, and she had a steadfast friend in Leslie. Not too shabby for a girl off a farm in Michigan.

One loose end. What role, if any, did Ivy have in the death of Jack Bauman? That matter was long since closed as far as the authorities were concerned. For Leslie it would always be a loose end. Ivy was the only witness to the event. Unless therapy loosened her memory of that evening, her role would remain unknown.

CHAPTER 100

The AllCare-Metro matter had evolved into a product liability case, likely to go on for years. Leslie's final story was written but without any reference to Alyssa Ross. The payola scheme was revealed but Eric Dillon's role in it was not confirmed.

Leslie had given up any hope of finding Luke Rollins. For her this was a huge disappointment. Identifying Luke as the hirer of the bagman and the killer of Lester Brandt had been the high point of her involvement in the AllCare case. Luke was the critical last witness in the saga.

Seeing the story end on that breakthrough was hard to take. Nevertheless, she knew when to fold up her tent and move on. She and her editor agreed they'd had a good run and it was now time to let this matter rest. Her wedding was just one month ahead so it wasn't as if she was desolate. Quite the contrary; a bright future lay ahead.

Luke had just disappeared. His long-divorced wife was the closest he had to a living relative but they had had no contact for several years.

Routine bills continued to be paid automatically out of his checking account. That account was kept solvent by automatic transfers from a bank money market account. There was no way of knowing how much cash he might have stashed away.

All indications suggested that Luke was either deceased, incapacitated, or just disinclined to resume his former life.

AllCare was besieged with product liability lawsuits seeking compensatory payment as more and more patients experienced premature failure of their artificial hip joints. Letitia Dillon, Eric's widow, was now the sole owner of the company. She was counseled to have AllCare seek bankruptcy protection as claims against the company mounted. Her mother agreed this was the best course of action.

Alyssa had lost behind-the-scenes control over a once very profitable business and a valuable means to launder funds generated by her drug business. More importantly though, she was escaping without any legal liability and was under no threat from the nosey reporter. With Luke Rollins gone the DA was disinclined to pursue the matter further. Alyssa believed Luke might never return but her effort to have him eliminated had been thwarted by his sudden disappearance.

CHAPTER 101

As a longtime associate of Alyssa Ross, Marjorie Bannister enjoyed many perks and a very comfortable lifestyle. Being a trusted insider gave her a sense of importance that stroked her ego. Now though, a faint ray of light revealed a small crack in the imaginary shield that distanced her from the unsavory actions emanating from the executive office. The distance was a delusion.

Luke Rollins was gone and she knew Alyssa had ordered his elimination. Failure to find him and carry out the directive was less relevant than the fact that a very trusted associate of Alyssa Ross had been deemed dispensable. The threesome of Luke, Alyssa, and herself had been the brain trust that she considered untouchable. Now she realized that Alyssa would defend herself at any cost and that included throwing her closest associates under the bus if need be.

Marge would be an invaluable witness in any investigation of Alyssa's role in the AllCare matter. Alyssa was certainly aware of that. Marge was no more secure than Luke Rollins and he'd gotten out just before the guillotine blade fell.

What recourse did she have? She might be willing to sign a nondisclosure agreement as part of her employment but a court could override the agreement if a judge decided it was shielding criminal activity.

She could put sensitive information in the hands of someone authorized to disclose the information in the event of her unnatural death. This would serve as a sort of insurance policy but it would put the threatening party on notice that a hostile action was contemplated. Her employment would likely end.

She could disappear, much as Luke had.

Lastly, she could make a preemptive strike and take out Alyssa before she, Marjorie, was eliminated. She wasn't confident that she could carry out a murder and get away with it.

As Marge considered these options she wondered if she wasn't being unduly unnerved by the imagined threat to her well-being. Was her situation that dire?

CHAPTER 102

Sitting in a comfortable easy chair, Luke Rollins watched the sun set behind the tenement across the street. Two months in a colorless rented apartment was beginning to wear on him. His disappearance from New York City and Ross-Wagner had been accomplished flawlessly. Now he contemplated his next move. He desperately wanted to rejoin the society he'd left behind; Philadelphia was not a bad place to hide out but it was not New York.

What was holding him back was the threat Alyssa had placed on his head. It surely hadn't expired. He still was a marked man and the only way he could see to remove the mark was to eliminate the person who set it in the first place.

The issue with the district attorney and his role as the fixer hinged on a highly unusual sketch artist's rendering in a lineup of similar drawings. This could be beaten in court. The problem was Alyssa Ross. She had to go.

His every waking hour was devoted to thinking through a plan to carry out a solution to his problem. Now he'd finally decided on a strategy and would move on to implementation. He picked up his phone and made a call.

Marge lived alone in a large, classy, Upper East Side apartment. Twice divorced, each dissolution had left her wealthier than before. She'd grown used to an empty apartment and was not interested in marrying a third time.

Sitting in bed, reading the current bestseller, she was

waiting for the evening news on TV to let viewers in on tomorrow's weather.

Her phone was next to the bed on its charger. A call this late in the evening would be highly unusual so the ringer was still active.

The ring startled her. Call waiting showed a number she didn't recognize. Normally, during the day, she'd ignore it, but at this hour she was curious enough to pick it up. She let the caller speak first.

"Hi, Marge. Don't faint. It's Luke. I'm very alive."

"Jesus. Is it really you, Luke? Just to be sure, what's my middle name?"

"Olivia. And your maiden name is Cummings. Are you satisfied?"

"Yes. Yes. Where the hell have you been these past few months, Luke? I guess I know *why* you went underground. At least I think I do."

"I think you do. That's why I'm coming to you live and not from the afterlife. You're the only person from my prior life that I've called. And I'd like to keep that a secret between just the two of us."

"I think you can trust me, Luke. I suspect there's something on your mind that's brought you back to life and makes me the first person on your call list."

"So right you are, Marge. Let's set up a meeting and I'll tell you what's on my mind. How about the Staten Island ferry terminal at ten a.m. tomorrow?"

"That works for me. Just dress warmly, Luke."

"Goodnight, Marge. It was good to hear your voice. Oh, one last thing. I now have a beard so don't be shocked when you see me."

CHAPTER 103

The ferry terminal was as cold as the street outside but the wind was kept out by the drafty walls. People milled about with scarves, gloves, and earmuffs while waiting for the ten thirty ferry to pull in.

Luke and Marjorie huddled in a protected corner of the large waiting room. Each was delighted to see the other.

"Thought I was really gone, didn't you Marge? I was not taking any chances with our mutual boss and colleague."

"I really did think you were taken out by her. How'd you escape in time?"

"I'll make it brief, Marge. The reporter we frequently discussed had a picture of me and was trying to affix my name to it. When the security guard at the Ross-Wagner building gave her my name he turned around and called me. I knew he'd tell Alyssa about the reporter and my picture. I took that as reason enough to disappear. Alyssa would put two and two together and see me as a liability she couldn't afford. That's it."

"Wow. That reporter certainly is as tenacious as Alyssa said she was. I'm glad you didn't hesitate to leave."

"That's in the past. Now I want to resume a normal life and not have to worry about a target on my back. You're up next, Marge. You just haven't been given liability status yet."

"I'm reading ahead, Luke. You want us to eliminate Alyssa before she can eliminate us. Is that why you called me?"

"Exactly. Now I want to tell you my plan. Your role will

not arouse any suspicion about you as a participant. You only have to help me gain access to Alyssa's office on an evening when she's working late. I have my old keys, but not one to Alyssa's office. I know all about the security system. After I carry out the deed, I'll stay in hiding for a month or so. Assuming there is no evidence incriminating me in the killing, I'll come back to life with a new identity and begin a normal existence."

"Okay. A minor role for me but in exchange for peace of mind."

CHAPTER 104

Access to the Ross-Wagner building was not difficult at night. Luke knew that the rear service door was rarely locked. Deliveries late at night or early morning were quite common so locking the entry could prove inconvenient for the reduced late hours staff. Luke waited for a brief period when the staff was fully occupied and made his entrance unnoticed.

The eight flights of stairs were easily mounted by his adrenalin charged body. The eighth -floor service door was not locked. Marjorie had done as he'd requested. Luke entered the familiar executive suite and headed down the hall to Alyssa's office.

He hesitated a moment outside her private backdoor exit and heard no voices. He drew his pistol, screwed on its silencer, took off the safety, and quickly entered the office.

Alyssa sat at her desk, focused on her computer screen. She looked up at him in shocked surprise. Before she could utter a word Luke shot her twice in the chest. The force of the shots sent her tumbling backward to the floor.

Luke peered over the desk and saw that both shots had hit her mid-chest. He removed the silencer and was about to replace the gun in his jacket pocket. Not until he turned to leave did he realize he was not alone.

Marge Bannister stood in the doorway to her adjoining office. Luke started to approach her but the gun in her hand stopped him.

"Sorry, Luke. I want a clean slate."

The first shot tore his left shoulder, the next hit him above the left eye. He was dead as soon as he hit the floor.

Marge calmly dialed 911.

CHAPTER 105

The evening's local news was full of buildings on fire, car crashes, and the occasional murder. Leslie paid it little attention while undressing for bed. Brad was involved in a late evening labor dispute and had called to indicate he'd be home after midnight.

When a familiar name came from the TV she immediately turned to the set and gave it her full attention. Alyssa Ross had been shot in her office. The news brief said the shooting had been reported around nine o'clock. The victim was transported to the emergency room at NYU Medical Center where she expired. There was no mention of a possible suspect.

Leslie was stunned. The story she'd put to sleep was suddenly very much alive. Her imagination was off and running. Who were the suspects? Who had a motive? And who had access to the very secure building? Who could enter and leave undetected?

Admittedly she didn't know every aspect of Alyssa's business life so enemies could be abundant. She did know All-Care and that was where her attention was directed.

With her wheels spinning rapidly only one person came to mind: Luke Rollins. Luke had a motive: self-preservation. He also must have had special access to the building and the executive offices. Luke would know the various ways to access the building and avoid detection.

One problem with this theory: Luke Rollins was nonexistent

If he now felt secure enough to resurface the police could arrest him for his role in the payola scheme and the murder of Lester Brandt. He could challenge the unorthodox lineup method used to ID him as the hirer of the bagman and Brandt's killer. Luke would be in the clear if his claim of misidentification held up in court. The DA wouldn't find the case compelling without being able to identify the person whose orders Luke or his look-alike were carrying out.

She let go of Luke for a moment. Was he the only one with that profile?

NO. One other person was a potential threat to Alyssa Ross. Her executive assistant, Marjorie Bannister. Maybe she hadn't been cast in that light, yet, but surely she knew it was just a matter of time before she'd step into Luke's shoes. If Alyssa was cleaning house, Marge would know she was near the top of the list for disposal.

Marge Bannister's motive was hypothetical and would be difficult to substantiate without knowing Alyssa's role, if any, in the AllCare scheme. Marge doubtless would have an alibi for the evening in question.

Absent these two suspects, Leslie could imagine no other candidate for the killing.

Now Leslie could see a more satisfying way to close out the AllCare story. Someone had breathed new life into it.

CHAPTER 106

Chan Young surveyed the scene of his third shooting of the day. Superficially, it seemed straightforward. The dead man on the floor shot the woman behind the desk with the still warm gun in his hand. The EMTs were struggling to extricate the woman on the floor behind the desk from the equipment she'd pulled down with her as she fell backward when two bullets hit her square in the middle of the chest. She was alive but one EMT said she was circling the drain.

A third person, female, sat calmly in a chair by the doorway leading to the adjoining office. She admitted shooting the man on the floor. In a brief interrogation she said she was the female victim's executive assistant and worked late next door when her boss did. She'd heard shots, grabbed the gun in her desk, and ran to the executive office. She'd come face-to-face with an armed man and shot him in self-defense.

Chan knew the story was never as simple as that.

Something was buzzing in his brain. The female victim's name had set off an alarm. He tried to recall where he'd heard it. Finally it clicked. Leslie Nugent and her complicated All-Care tale.

CHAPTER 107

A call from Chan Young at this late hour was unusual and got Leslie's immediate attention. At first she was all ears. AllCare had come to life once again and Chan wanted her help in sorting out the characters at the scene of a shooting. She couldn't say no to this invitation.

"Be there in half an hour."

Half an hour was a good estimate. A police officer let her off the elevator on the eighth floor in less than that. Chan quickly summarized the crime scene. It seemed obvious that the bearded man lying dead on the floor had shot Ross. The barrel of the gun in his hand was still warm. His identity was a mystery.

Chan related the information offered by the only living eyewitness. She could not identify the man she'd shot.

Leslie eyed the dead man and was unsure of his identity. Unsure but not without a suspicion.

"I'd like to see him clean-shaven after you photograph him bearded, of course. The beard is a distraction. I don't want to mislead you with a misidentification."

"I can take care of the photos and the shave. The rescue truck has the necessary equipment."

Chan called down to his team on the ground floor and in twenty minutes the dead man was clean-shaven.

"I think this is Luke Rollins, Chan. I never met him but I have a good picture of him that several others have been able to agree is a good likeness. Assuming it's him, that makes the threesome you encountered here quite interesting. Let's move out into the hall where Ms. Bannister can't hear us."

They did as Leslie suggested and she wasted no time trying to make sense of the maddening coincidence that brought these three coworkers together for one last fatal encounter.

"Chan, I think I have this scene figured out. I see one person emerging as the winner. Obviously, the dead man and his victim are losers but Bannister is a big winner. She comes away with no one in a position to incriminate her in any of the nefarious acts planned in this office. Rollins was probably trying to get a target off his back by eliminating Ross. He succeeded but didn't reckon with Bannister doing to him what he was doing to Ross: eliminating him as a potential witness against her. So, she's in the clear now; the last man standing has eliminated the last possible witness against her. Luke gave her the cover she needed to eliminate him. It sounds plausible as I hear myself spout it out but I don't know if it's provable."

"It sounds plausible, Leslie, but it's laden with conjecture. It's obviously not the story Bannister tells. In her version she was responding to gunfire and found herself confronted by a stranger with a gun in his hand. Simple as that. You had trouble recognizing the shooter so it's not a far stretch she might have had the same problem facing the bearded assassin."

Leslie nodded in agreement. At least now she knew Luke Rollins had been alive these past few months. The All-Care story was coming to an end since all the players were accounted for. Marjorie Bannister was the one loose end but she wasn't a key player.

CHAPTER 108

John Livingstone and Leslie had agreed that one more turn of the wheel was justified. The AllCare story would be exhumed briefly for the reporter to interview Marjorie Bannister, assuming she would give one. Alyssa's death, and Luke's, left a lingering suspicion in Leslie's mind that Marge had defended herself better than appeared on the surface.

Leslie saw Luke as a potential witness against Marjorie in two capacities: first, as a coconspirator in Alyssa's murder, and second, as a colleague consorting with Alyssa and himself in a host of illegal acts.

She'd conspired with Luke to eliminate Alyssa but at the last minute saw a way to wipe her slate clean. That was bothersome.

Marjorie Bannister agreed to an interview in her office.

Leslie was welcomed into Marge's office with a warm smile. This was a more friendly greeting than she'd experienced the last time.

Her dress and demeanor showed no sign of grief over the recent death of her close colleagues.

Leslie was shown into the office and was ushered to a comfortable easy chair. Marge seated herself directly opposite.

"So, Leslie, you didn't tell me why we're having this unexpected interview. Alyssa's death stunned everyone who knew her. I'm sure that's the reason for the interview but I can't see how I'm tied in."

"I'm not sure you are, Marge. I just wanted to hear your

response to some of my suspicions. I gave a lot of thought to Alyssa's murder and could only think of two people who had a motive for the killing: Luke Rollins and *you*. Luke was an existential threat to Alyssa and may have been earmarked for elimination. He would have fled for his safety. You possessed the same incriminating information he did but were not on Alyssa's hit list. Not yet."

Marge's welcoming smile had faded. Her new expression was cold and unrevealing. She placed her phone on the coffee table between them and turned on the record mode. She made no effort to conceal her intention to record the interview.

"This has to be all off the record, Leslie. Otherwise, our conversation will be over before it begins."

"That's fair. I'm only trying to find out if my suspicions hold any water."

"In that case, I assume we're off the record and the recorder can verify that."

"I'm fine with that, Marge. I'm not here to trick you."

"Getting back to your suspicion regarding Alyssa's murder, I have no information about Luke's motive. I only know that I saw a smoking weapon in the hand of a bearded stranger and shot him before he could use the weapon on me. I didn't recognize him initially.

"I believe Alyssa had him tagged for elimination when she learned about the picture you had in your possession. He and Alyssa worked very close to each other. His identification in connection with some highly illegal activities posed a very real threat to her."

"So, you were aware of the manner of his identification and its implication?"

"Yes, Alyssa didn't keep much secret from me. Luke's ID separated him from me as a damaging witness. Let me be clear, Leslie; a lot of bad moves came out of Alyssa's office. Luke and I had a hand in crafting many of them and for that I'm truly sorry. Alyssa was our leader and she inherited her father's ruthlessness when it came to dealing with people who threatened her.

"I'm trying to undo her influence on this organization. My plan is to help her daughter run this company, free of her mother's base instincts. That'll be my penitence. I'm quite serious about that."

Leslie didn't let Marge steer the conversation away from her focus on the murder. "And elimination of Alyssa was the first step in that direction?"

"I understand where you're coming from, Leslie, but I won't go there. Alyssa's death ended a sordid chapter in the history of Ross-Wagner. I see a new chapter beginning and will try to bury the past. There's nothing to gain from digging up any dirt. These are the last words I have for you; let it rest."

Marge stood up, indicating their meeting was over. The women walked out to the elevator.

"I understand your position, Marge. And maybe I'll take your advice. There's a lot more story to tell but I don't see any benefit in pursuing it further. Thanks for your time, Marge."

They smiled at each other as the elevator door closed.

Waiting for the doorman to snag a cab, Leslie reflected on what little she'd learned from Marge. A lot of badness had transpired in the AllCare mess, including several human casualties. Marge had made no effort to whitewash Alyssa and her mode of operation. Her own contrition, though, didn't ring true.

She'd wait and watch. There were other stories to pursue. This one had run its course and the lone survivor considered herself in the clear and untethered to a gloomy past.

EPILOGUE

Nonstop, first class to Rome was a terrific wedding present from Brad's parents. The wedding had gone off without a hitch and the couple was now relaxing at thirty thousand feet with flutes of champagne.

AllCare was fading into the distant past. Leslie's attention was focused on her future with Brad and the upcoming two weeks in Rome, Florence, and Venice.

John Livingstone had sent her off after her final story filing on AllCare. He admonished her to clear her brain, come back refreshed, and be ready for new challenges.

The AllCare saga had begun simply enough with her mother's premature hip prosthesis failure. It had evolved into a large, illegal monopoly scheme with a number of casualties. She'd almost been one of them. Now it was over and she'd extracted as much copy as she could before the story ran out of gas.

Done.

ABOUT THE AUTHOR

A.S. Most is a retired cardiologist with a passion for mystery/thrillers. Harlan Coben and Michael Connelly are among his favorite authors. *A Bribe Turns Lethal* is Most's fourth novel. He is also the author of *No Loose Ends*, *A Deadly Cover*, and *The Sniper*. Most resides in Rhode Island with his artist/educator wife. He has two sons, one an attorney and the other a journalist. He is actively working on his fifth book.